Cameron
Meets Madison

JACK WEYLAND

Published and Distributed by:

PUBLISHING & DISTRIBUTION L.L.C.

Granite Publishing and Distributions, LLC
868 North 1430 West
Orem, UT 84057
(801) 229-9023 Toll Free (800) 574-5779
www.granitebooks.com

Cover Design by Lizabeth Rolfson
Page Layout and Design by Myrna M. Varga

ISBN: 978-1-59936-054-6
Library of Congress Control Number: 2010924482

First Printing: April 2010

1 3 5 7 9 10 8 6 4 2

Printed in the United States of America

Cameron Meets Madison

CHAPTER ONE

Have you ever had a day that was so good you wished it would never end? I used to have those too.

Not anymore.

Today is going to be such a great day! I thought as I walked into the foyer of Lincoln High the Monday after our team won the state football title the previous Friday night.

The halls were crowded with everyone hurrying to class, and I couldn't help but notice how many of them were looking at me. "Hey, great game, Cameron!" some guy called out as I headed for my locker.

"Thanks, but actually it was a team effort," I said, trying to sound modest. My mom was always lecturing me about that.

"That's not the way it looked to me," the guy said. "Especially your last touchdown."

I nodded. He was, of course, right. And even though I was used to that kind of praise, it was still good to hear.

I was still recovering from partying Saturday night, and I stopped at a drinking fountain to down a couple of aspirin.

Madison, a girl who worked for the school paper was waiting for me at my locker. She'd interviewed me the Monday before our big game and was back now for a follow-up interview.

MY FIRST INTERVIEW with Madison had been a disaster. She'd cornered me in the hall after practice as team members were leaving the locker room. Unfortunately they were the audience I was playing to.

As the quarterback and leader of our team, I felt it important to reflect a winning attitude. Included in that was the expectation that every girl in school should adore me. Even a girl like Madison, in her off-white shirt, buttoned to the top, and her pleated tan slacks. This girl dressed more like a school librarian than an actual student.

She was obviously not the kind of girl I'd ever be interested in. But the truth is the guys on the team had certain expectations, and I couldn't let them down. I had to make it look to them as though I was totally irresistible to this girl, too. Otherwise, how could they have the kind of confidence in me they needed during a game?

She and I sat down on a bench outside the locker room for the interview. She took out a notebook and a pen. "What is the team doing this week to get ready for Friday night's championship game?"

As they walked by us, the fullback and one of the tight ends stopped to watch me with this girl. I had a reputation to uphold, and the pressure was on.

"Coach Grogan said for us to just relax. Speaking of relaxing, you want to relax with me in my car? We could play some music."

My teammates smirked as they walked past us.

She frowned. "Let's just get this over with, okay? I know you're busy."

"Yeah, sure. Well, to answer your question, mainly, like today, we just went back over the basics. Coach says all we have to do Friday is to do what got us to this point. Why mess with something that's not broken?"

She wrote that down.

"How do you keep from being nervous?" she asked.

Three other players, on their way out, stopped to see what I was up to.

"You know what?" I said for their benefit, "I'm too busy this week to see you, but maybe I could work you in next week. Thanks for asking. Also, you don't need to pay for dinner too."

They nodded their approval and high-fived me. "Tell her about your bet!" the fullback asked.

"What bet?" she asked.

"He bet the team that he can kiss all the cheerleaders by next Monday." With that, he and the bunch of guys he was with walked off, leaving us alone again.

She glared at me and set her pad of paper down. "What is wrong with you?" she asked.

"Nothing. It's not for me, it's for the team. So they'll have confidence in me."

She stood up. "You know what? I don't need this interview that much. Have a nice day," she said as she started to walk away.

I didn't care much what someone like her thought about me. But even so, I didn't want her writing bad things about me for the school paper because some girls I actually liked might believe it, and that wouldn't be good for my social life.

So I caught up with her. "Look, I'm sorry for being such a jerk. It's just the pressure of the game on Friday, that's all. It's making me do things I'd never do normally. Give me another chance, okay?"

She hesitated.

"Please," I said.

"Okay. But I don't want to be alone with you. So any interview we do has to be someplace where there are other people around."

The library was still open so we ended up in there.

We sat down at a table, and she got out her notepad again and asked me a few questions about what it's like to be out on the field, playing in front of all those people and how we decide what we're going to run.

When I started to tell her about how easy it is to get hurt playing football, she laughed. "How could you get hurt wearing all that armor?"

"Pads. They're called pads."

"Okay, pads. Seems a little sissy-like, though."

"Hey, you don't know what it's like to have a bunch of two-hundred-pound guys piling on you," I complained.

She wasn't impressed. "Poor little guy."

I could have gotten mad, but I wanted to stay on her good side. I looked at her for a moment, and then said, "I know I've seen you around."

"We were in a class together about a year ago."

"Oh, yeah, that's it," I said, as though I remembered.

"Do you remember what class it was?" she asked.

"Actually, no. Sorry."

"American History."

"Well, it was a big class."

"I sat right behind you," she said.

"You've changed your hair since then, right?" I asked.

"No."

"Lost some weight?"

"No."

I gave it another try. "Got contacts?"

"Look, it's okay if you don't remember me."

"I remember you, mostly."

"It's okay. Everyone in school knows your name, but you can't possibly know all of us. Tell me, is it hard to be you?" she asked with a slightly mocking tone to her voice.

"No, it's easy. Remind me again what your name is."

"Madison."

"Oh, sure. Madison. I remember you now."

She didn't believe me. "Yeah, right."

I held up my hand. "No, wait, give me a minute! I actually do remember you! You gave me . . . uh . . . like a Christmas card. With a picture of Jesus. And there was something about a free DVD."

She actually smiled. "Well, I'm impressed. Did you ever call the toll-free number?"

"No, not really, but I still have the card . . . somewhere."

"Well, you can still make the call."

"Right. And I will, real soon in fact."

She shrugged. "It's up to you."

"So, you're like religious?" I asked.

"Yeah, pretty much. I belong to The Church of Jesus Christ of Latter-day Saints. Some people call us Mormons, I guess because of another book of scripture we have in addition to the Bible. It's called the Book of Mormon."

"What's that like? Being a Mormon?"

"Do you really want to know? Or are you making fun of me?"

"No. I'm interested. What's up with being a Mormon?"

She studied me for a moment, as though she was trying to decide what to do, then began a kind of recitation: " 'We believe in God, the Eternal Father, and in his son Jesus Christ, and in the Holy Ghost. We believe . . . ' "

She just kept going, like it was something she'd memorized. This was way more than I wanted to know, but I let her go on because I wanted her to write a good story about me. I had no interest in what she was saying, but there was no doubt about her enthusiasm.

She wrapped it up with: " 'We believe in being honest, true, chaste, benevolent, virtuous, and in doing good to all men; indeed, we may say that we follow the admonition of Paul—We believe all things, we hope all things, we have endured many things, and hope to be able to endure all things. If there is anything virtuous, lovely, or of good report or praiseworthy, we seek after these things.' "

I'd never met anyone like her before. She reminded me of religious people they make fun of on late night TV. But with her it wasn't something I felt like ridiculing. She was so . . . well . . . sincere. One thing was clear, though: she wasn't someone I'd have any interest in. We were way too different.

After she finished telling me what Mormons believe, I nodded. "That's you, isn't it?" I asked.

"What's me?"

"Virtuous and lovely."

She shrugged. "I don't know. I don't spend much time thinking about that."

"I've never used the word *lovely* before in my life. But, you know what? It fits you. You're the kind of girl my mom would like."

She stood up. "Well, thanks for your time. And good luck Friday night. If it's all right, I'd like to interview you next Monday, too."

"Yeah, sure, no problem. Will you be at the game?"

"Actually, I will. I play in the pep band."

"Oh, yeah, well . . . I actually don't know anyone in the pep band."

"Now you do."

"I guess so."

She was ready to leave, but she had me wondering about her. "So," I asked, "how do the things you believe affect how you live your life?"

She thought about it as we walked out of the library then said, "My folks have always taught me that we're here on earth to serve others."

"Well, that's a different way of looking at life."

She looked into my eyes. "Also, I know that God lives and that we are his children," she said.

"Well, that's good," I said like I even cared.

"How do you look at life?" she asked.

"The way I see it, we're here to succeed in everything we do. That's why I'm so competitive."

As we approached the door leading out of the school, a girl and a guy were waiting for her. They both looked as though they came from a home without much money. The girl had a few things going for her, mainly blue eyes and long red hair, and she was tall for a girl, which I liked. But unfortunately I had to deduct points because of the *Nemo* lunch box sticking out of her backpack. I didn't know anyone who brought their lunch to school. My guess was that her family was so poor that she packed peanut butter and jelly sandwiches for lunch. And who can respect that, right?

"Sorry, I was so late," Madison said. "I had to do an interview."

"That's okay. We knew you'd come," the girl said.

Madison introduced us. "This is Cameron. He's the quarterback on the football team. Cameron, this is Emma Jean and her brother, Toby. They're friends of mine."

"I can't believe I'm meeting you!" Emma Jean gushed.

"Yeah, I know," I said.

Toby was slight in build and looked like he never had enough to eat. His sandy brown hair looked like he hadn't washed it in a month, and he kept his head down, to avoid eye contact, I guessed.

Alexis, one of the most popular girls in school, stopped to talk to me on her way out of school. She had a stack of flyers in her hand. "Cameron, after you guys win Friday night, we're having a celebration party on Saturday night. It'll be at my folks' cabin. They'll be out of town. Oh, here's the directions." She handed me a flyer. "You'll be there, right?"

"Yeah. That sounds great."

Emma Jean stepped forward. "Can I have a flyer too?" she asked.

Alexis didn't see me shaking my head, so she gave Emma Jean one of the flyers. And then she left.

I didn't want to be seen with Emma Jean, Toby, and Madison, so I told them I'd forgotten something in my locker. I stayed inside until they left.

That was the first interview I had with Madison.

BACK TO THE MONDAY morning after the game with Madison

waiting for me at my locker.

"Can we do a follow-up interview now?" she asked. "I know you'll be busy later on. Especially with the victory rally this afternoon." She pulled out her notebook. "This is a big day for you, isn't it?"

"Not just for me. It's a big day for the entire school."

"Okay," she said, but in a tone of voice that sounded like she didn't actually believe it. "I just have a couple of questions." She looked at her notes. "For you, personally, what was it like to win the state football title?"

"It's not just that we won. It's the way we won that's so important. We were trailing by four points with only thirty seconds on the clock. Fourth and nine. If we don't score, then we lose. There are some important lessons you can learn in situations like that."

She scribbled something down. "Such as?"

"Like never giving up and making good use of the time you've got left."

She raised her hand to stop me so she could get down what I'd said. "Sorry, I'm a little slow . . . 'making good use . . . of the time . . . you've got left.' Okay, got it."

She asked a few more questions and scribbled down my answers. Five minutes later she closed her notebook. "I think I'm done. Thanks for your time."

"Did you see me make the last touchdown?"

"Ah, well, no, it was so late in the game, and it was raining. The pep band was on our way to the bus. Actually, I don't usually pay much attention to the game. We get to talking, you know—"

"Well, you missed a great play. I ran forty yards for a touchdown."

"And became a football hero in the process, right?"

"This is not about me, okay? This win is important for the entire school. Even for, you know, people like you."

"Okay," she said without much enthusiasm.

"See, the thing is, the team and I did this so that even people who don't care that much about football can be proud to be a Lincoln High School Eagle."

She glanced at the clock. "Actually, I need to get to class."

"You don't believe I did this for the school?"

"Not really, but that's okay, right? It doesn't matter what I think."

"Tell me why you think that."

She took a deep breath and looked at me for a few moments before saying, "When I sat behind you in class, the only people you talked to were two cheerleaders and a guy who was on the team with you. You completely ignored the rest of us."

"Now I can see I made a big mistake not paying attention to you."

"Give me a break, okay? You don't care about me. Look, the point is that everybody in school is important and deserves respect. Not just the guys on the football team."

"You sound like my mom," I muttered.

"Your mom's right."

"I respect people."

A guy came up to me and slapped me on the back. "Hey, you guys rocked Friday night!"

"Thanks."

"I heard you bet the team last Monday that you could kiss every cheerleader by today. Is that true?"

I glanced at Madison. She was frowning, but I didn't care that much what she thought about me.

I nodded. "You know what? I did it, too! I won the bet!"

"In one week? How many cheerleaders are there?"

"Ten."

"And you kissed all ten of them in a week? How'd you ever do that?"

I flashed him my winning smile. "What can I say? Girls can't resist me."

"Awesome! The state championship and now this! What a guy!" He lightly slugged me on the shoulder and then left.

Madison scowled and shook her head.

"Look, it's not like it sounds."

"Yeah, right. Tell me one more time that you did it for the team," she said sarcastically.

"Well the truth is I did."

She brushed past me. "Excuse me. I need to get to class."

I walked beside her. "Let me explain, okay? This was my way to get the team focused on something other than the big game coming up. You know, so we wouldn't feel the pressure of playing for the state title. I made the bet mainly for the team's benefit. It's the kind of leadership you need from a good quarterback."

She glared at me. "You know what? You're totally pathetic."

"The thing is, it worked. Last week in the locker room before and after practice, that's all they talked about. So it accomplished what I wanted it to do."

"And how are those girls going to feel when they find out you kissed them just because of some dumb bet you made with the team?"

"I don't know. Flattered, I guess. I mean, let's face it, I am the best quarterback in the state."

She shook her head and walked faster.

I kept up with her. "It wasn't like what you must be thinking. Friday night, right after the game, everyone was out on the field celebrating. Whenever I saw one of the cheerleaders, I gave her a hug and a kiss on the cheek. And then I thanked her for all she'd done for the team during the season. I did that with all of the cheerleaders. So, really, if you think about it, it was just my way of showing my appreciation to them. Also, except for one girl, it was just a kiss on the cheek. And with that girl, it was totally her idea, not mine. So it's not like, you know, I'm some kind of a conceited jerk."

"Of course not. You did it for the school! And also for your inflated opinion of yourself." She stopped in front of her classroom. "The paper will be coming out on Wednesday. If you want, I can save you some extra copies so you can hang them all over your room. Or you can give an autographed copy to all the cheerleaders and to all the other girls you happen to make out with in the next few days."

"You know what? I probably won't even look at the paper . . . but my mom will want a few extra copies."

"No problem. I'll save twenty of them for you. You can pick them up at the office. Thank you for the interview."

"I'll give you a call," I said.

She shook her head. "What for? I think we're done here."

As I watched her leave, I was a little disappointed. Girls usually liked me. Well, at least when I first meet a girl, she usually likes me. Not so much later on, though.

I had more important things to think about than worry what some random girl like her thought about me. More important things, like reliving in my mind what a great game I'd had Friday night.

WE PLAYED THE STATE championship game in a domed stadium at a university twenty miles away.

In the fourth quarter, with only thirty seconds on the clock, fourth down, we were trailing 13–9 with nine yards to go for a first down. The ball was on the other team's forty-yard line.

I took the snap, dropped back, and looked for an open receiver. Just after I threw the ball, a defensive lineman broke free and started barreling toward me.

I overthrew the ball and it sailed out of bounds.

The game should have been over. But the defensive lineman was still coming toward me. I turned away from him and ran like I still had the ball.

The referee blew the play dead just before the lineman crashed into me full speed, knocking me down.

Even though I knew I was going to get hit and had braced for the collision, it still hurt, and I didn't get up right away.

The referee threw his flag. "Personal foul. Fifteen-yard penalty. Repeat fourth down."

That gave us one more chance to win the game. On the next play, I sent all my receivers running down-field. I pump-faked once, twice, and then seeing that all my receivers were covered, I began to run.

For a brief instant, Jorge Gonzales, running along the sidelines, was open. The only problem was I didn't know him very well. His family had just moved to town in the summer. Before that he'd played football in California. He was good, but the coach hadn't played him much until our game a week earlier when one of our starting wide-outs had been injured.

My first instinct was to throw the ball to Gonzales for an easy touchdown, but because he was so new on our squad, I wasn't sure if he'd be able to catch it. I waited too long and the next second he was covered too, and it was too late to make the throw.

With the field spread, I spotted an open lane. There was a small chance I could run it in for a touchdown.

The first twenty yards were easy because the other team was in a deep-pass defense. But then things started to get tough. I straight-armed one guy, dodged another, stopped, reversed direction, and then saw an opening and ran the ball in for a touchdown.

The game was over! And we'd won!

It got crazy after that. My teammates hoisted me on their shoulders and paraded me around the field.

Just before they put me down, one of the guys on the team reminded me of my bet. So, naturally, being a competitive guy, I went into action.

A few minutes later I realized I'd only kissed nine, but there were ten cheerleaders. I asked one of the cheerleaders which girl was missing.

"Jasmine. She hurt her foot during one of her jumps. She's having the trainer look at it."

"Where'd they go? I have to find her."

"They left the field."

I looked all over for her, but I couldn't find her.

I decided to fake it. In the locker room when I reminded the team they would be taking me out for pizza next week, someone asked, "You didn't kiss Jasmine, though, did you? She wasn't even on the field at the end of the game."

"Oh, well then, maybe not."

"Then you lost. Too bad. Buying pizza for all us guys is going to cost you a bundle."

"I've got until Monday."

"You'll never do it."

"Oh, I will. I always achieve every goal I set."

They laughed and had a huge argument over where we ought to go for pizza.

On Saturday night I went to Alexis's victory party outside of town.

I asked around and found out that Jasmine was planning to come to the party.

Since I barely knew her, I decided that when she first walked in, I'd run over to her like I was still pumped up over our big victory and give her a hug and a kiss on the cheek, like it was all spontaneous.

I learned much later that because of her sprained ankle it had taken her several minutes to limp from the car into the cabin.

I ran over to her, picked her up in my arms, and whirled her around. "Jasmine, we won! We won! Thanks for getting the fans behind us."

Unfortunately, as I was whirling her around, her bad ankle smacked into the edge of the kitchen table, and she screamed out in pain.

I could see my opportunities were fast ending, so while she was sobbing, I kissed her on the cheek.

"What are you doing?" she yelled through her tears.

"I was overcome by my excitement that we won the game."

"Can't you see she's in pain?" another cheerleader asked.

"Oh, yeah, I can see that now."

"And why did you pick her up and fling her around? You knew she had a sprained ankle, right? And why did you kiss her?"

"Uh, I guess it was just my excitement at seeing her, and, you know, because of what a great job the cheerleaders did to help us win."

That seemed to make things better—for about ten seconds. And then one of the more stupid team members said, "Good job, Cam! You won the bet! When do you want us to pay up?"

"What are you talking about?" the same annoying cheerleader asked.

"Cameron bet the team he could kiss every cheerleader in a week. He kissed all of you except for Jasmine after the game, so she was the only one he had left to kiss."

The cheerleaders gathered menacingly around me.

"Actually, I did it for the team," I said lamely.

"You are such a low-life jerk!" the annoying one yelled at me.

"No, I'm not. Not really."

The cheerleaders helped Jasmine out to the car and then they all drove away. Actually, a lot of girls left with them, so the only girls who were left were those that I didn't even care about. Like Emma Jean. I don't know who gave her a ride out to the cabin. She wasn't friends with anybody else there.

I spent the rest of the night on the couch watching highlights of the game with anyone who cared to see it.

By one-thirty in the morning most of the girls had left, except for Emma Jean. I'd totally ignored her while I was surrounded by people I actually liked, but now that all of them had left, she became slightly more interesting to me.

I slid closer to her, put my arm around her, and kissed her. Because of who I was, she seemed flattered by the attention. Who could blame her, right?

Ten minutes later, Alexis saw the last of her friends off at the door and then returned to the living room. "Cameron, everyone else has gone. You two are welcome to stay, but I'm going to bed."

"Okay, goodnight."

I went into the kitchen and grabbed myself another beer. By the time I sat down again beside her, Emma Jean had fallen asleep.

With her beside me snoring, I drank my beer and once again watched highlights of the game. After a while, I fell asleep too.

Early the next morning, Alexis ran down the stairs and into the living room. "Wake up! My folks are back in town and they're coming up here! Help me pick up all these empty beer cans, okay?"

I had a huge headache, but when Emma Jean got up to help, I did too. Alexis asked me if I could take the trash bag with the beer cans with me so her folks wouldn't see them.

"Yeah, okay," I said, on my way out the door with a garbage bag.

"Can you give me a ride home?" Emma Jean asked.

I pretended that I hadn't heard her.

"Please. I don't have any other way to get home, and it's too far to walk."

I paused.

Alexis came to her rescue. "Cameron, what is wrong with you? Give her a ride home."

Emma Jean and I got in the car and started down the gravel road.

"I can give you my phone number if you want," she said.

I shrugged. "Whatever."

She scribbled it down on a scrap of paper and gave it to me. I stuffed it into my shirt pocket.

Emma Jean was acting all nervous. "My mom is going to wonder why I never came home last night," she whined.

"Tell her that you were at some friends' and you were watching highlights of the championship game and everyone fell asleep."

"Actually, that is what happened," she said.

"Oh, yeah, I guess it is."

"Toby won't believe I was with you last night."

"I can hardly believe it either," I mumbled sarcastically. My head was still pounding, and the last thing I wanted was to listen to her jabbering.

"The three of us have the same lunch period. Maybe I could bring him by to get you to sign his football."

"Don't bring him around until I've given you permission."

"It's that house there."

I pulled into her driveway. It was a small one-story house in need of paint.

Emma Jean seemed to be waiting for something.

"You getting out or not?" I asked.

"Aren't you going to walk me to the door?"

"No, I'm too tired. Just go, okay?"

"We're friends now, right?"

"Yeah, right," I scoffed. "We're totally inseparable."

"Call me, okay?"

"Would you please just get out of the stupid car?" I yelled.

She pursed her lips, nodded, opened the door, and hurried up the walk to her house.

I drove home, woke up my folks, and told them I'd fallen asleep with some friends watching a movie. They seemed okay with that.

A few minutes later I crawled into bed.

I slept most of Sunday and then ate dinner with my folks. Our neighbor had recorded our local sports channel's coverage of the big game so I watched it with my mom and dad.

After a couple of times watching the clip, they left to go shopping, but I stayed behind and watched it over and over again.

I was definitely a sports hero. You know what? That's about as good as it gets.

AFTER MADISON INTERVIEWED me for the paper on Monday following our big win, I reported to Coach Grogan's office.

None of the football players had a first-period class. It was Coach's way of checking up on us, making sure we were in school every day and that we were keeping up in all our classes. All we had to do was drop by his office and get our names checked off. After that we were free to do whatever.

The team usually ended up hanging out in the room where they stored the wrestling mats. Coach had given me the key to the room. Mostly we'd sit around and talk until the bell rang for second period.

Gonzales, as usual, sat by himself and studied.

I walked over and sat next to him. "Studying?"

He nodded.

"On that last play, you were open. I should've thrown you the ball."

"It turned out okay."

"Yeah, it did. What are you going to do after you graduate?"

"Earn money for college."

"I bet you could get a scholarship to play ball in college."

He shook his head. "We've moved around too much. Nobody knows how good I am."

I felt a little guilty. If I'd thrown him the ball and if he'd caught it and run it in for a touchdown, he would've gotten a little press and maybe had a better chance of getting a football scholarship.

I stood up. "Well, something will turn out. It always does, right?"

He looked up at me. "Does it?"

No wonder you have no friends, I thought. I returned to be with my friends.

"Who was that girl you were with Saturday night?" my friend Wade asked. Wade and I had played sports together since sixth grade.

I shrugged. "Nobody important."

"That's Emma Jean," the fullback said. "I had her in class once. She's such a loser. So what did the two of you do after the rest of us left?"

"Nothin'."

"Don't give us that. We all know better. Tell us what happened."

I didn't care anything about Emma Jean. And I didn't want to disappoint my teammates. So I improvised. "The truth is she couldn't get enough of me."

"I knew it!"

Over the next few minutes, they kept suggesting things we might have done. I just smiled and said, "I'm not going to tell you that." Which to them meant we'd done whatever it was they had suggested.

It was in the middle of my ten o'clock class that I began to worry that rumors about me and Emma Jean might make me look bad to girls I actually liked.

After class, I talked to one of the guys on the team. "I want what happened between Emma Jean and me to be kept just within the team. Have you told anyone?"

"Well, yeah, but just a couple of guys."

"Don't tell anyone else, okay? And if you see any of the guys, tell them not to tell anyone either, okay?"

"Yeah, sure."

Unfortunately, in a couple of hours the news about me and Emma Jean had spread throughout the school.

I had a test in my eleven o'clock class over chapters I hadn't read. My teacher, Mrs. Arnold, noticed me staring into space while I waited for everyone else to finish.

"You haven't studied for this test, have you?" she asked.

"I've been busy, Mrs. Arnold. Some of us have lives."

"Don't expect any favors from me just because you're a jock."

"I don't."

"I know this is hard for you to see now, but life is more than sports."

"Maybe for you, it is, but not for me. In four or five years, I expect to be making over a million dollars a year playing in the NFL. That's what my future holds for me. What does it hold for you, Mrs. Arnold?"

She looked as though she was about to cry and quickly turned away. I wasn't expecting that because she was usually as hard as nails. She walked to her desk, grabbed a tissue, and left the room.

What's that all about? I thought.

At noon I ate lunch with the team. It was great to be with them again and talk about the game. In the middle of our celebration, Madison approached me. "Can I talk to you?" she asked.

"You need a picture? Take it of all of us because it was a team effort."

She shook her head. "I don't need a picture. I need to talk to you."

"Yeah, sure."

We went into the hall.

"I've heard some rumors about you and Emma Jean. Is it true what people are saying?"

I sighed. "Nothing happened. We were both at a party Saturday night. That's all."

"So you made up lies about her and you?"

"I never actually said we did anything."

"Then where did all the rumors come from?"

"How should I know?"

"You know, don't you? Tell me."

"Why should I tell you anything?"

"Don't you even care what this will do to Emma Jean?"

"Look on the bright side. Maybe now she'll be more popular with guys."

"What is wrong with you? You don't even know how stupid that sounds. You don't care about anyone but yourself. People say what a big football hero you are, but you're no hero of mine." She walked away.

I caught up with her. "Okay, look, I admit that I messed up. I never should've let this go on. But there's nothing I can do about it now."

"At the rally, you could tell everyone that there've been some rumors going around school about you that aren't tru . You wouldn't even have to say Emma Jean's name. At least that would be something."

"I'm not going to do that. The rally is supposed to be a time of celebration for our team and for the school."

"You have nothing to celebrate, Cameron."

"Hey, don't make such a big deal out of it, okay? In a few days nobody will even remember this. Time always makes things better."

"You don't care that Emma Jean will carry this stigma for the rest of her life, do you?"

"To be honest, no. I don't really care what happens to her."

Madison stormed away, and I returned to my friends in the cafeteria.

"What did that girl want?" Wade asked as I sat back down at the table.

"It was just about something she's writing for the school paper."

A few minutes later, while I was eating my dessert, Toby came to our table. "What do you want, kid?"

"I need to talk to you," he said softly.

"Go ahead and talk. Devin, go over and ask Megan if she wants her dessert."

"How come she always gives you her dessert?" Devin asked.

"She's anorexic, so giving me part of her lunch works out for both of us."

Toby was still standing there.

"If you've got something to say, say it," I told him.

He cleared his throat and looked at me. He had sad eyes. "Emma Jean just left school crying. Why are you telling lies about her?"

All my friends at the table were watching to see what I'd do. "Who says they're lies?" I said.

"Emma Jean is not that kind of girl."

I grinned. "Let me tell you something, dude. All girls are that kind of girl if you get 'em in the right situation."

"You mean like alone with you, right, Cameron?" Wade asked.

I smiled. "Well, I hate to brag."

"You lied about my sister!" Toby shouted. ·

"That's a pretty serious charge. You want to take this outside?"

Toby looked like he might cry, but his jaws were clenched tight. "Yes, I do."

Devin returned with Megan's pudding. I stood up, grabbed Toby's arm, took the bowl of pudding, plopped it upside down on top of his head, removed the dish, and rubbed the pudding into his hair. All the guys at our table thought it was funny and started laughing.

"Listen, runt. Don't ever come around here again," I said.

Toby tried to hit me, but I caught his fist in mid-air, turned him around, and marched him out of the cafeteria to an empty locker next to mine. I shoved him into the locker, closed it, and braced my hand on the locker so he couldn't get out.

Toby didn't say anything at first, but after a few moments, he said, "Please let me out."

"Promise not to bother me again?"

"I'm not promising anything. You lied about Emma Jean."

I paused. "Okay, look, even if that's true, there's nothing I can do about it now."

"She says she's never coming back to school."

"Okay, so she's the rumor of the day, but don't worry, it'll all blow over in a few days. The thing is, you're starting to make me mad. Say you'll leave me alone, or you'll be in there all day."

"I'm not promising anything. I don't care if I die in here."

That worried me. I opened the locker and let him out. "Go wash your hair, Toby. It's a mess. And don't ever come around me again."

When I returned to my friends in the cafeteria, one of them asked, "So what did you do to Pudding Head?"

"I shoved him in a locker and kept him there until he started bawling like a girl. It was totally pathetic."

"You and Emma Jean did have a good time on Saturday night, like you said, right?"

"Absolutely. Just like we talked about. You can count on it."

I skipped my one o'clock class to get ready for the pep rally. Wade and I got the trophy out of the coach's office and took it to the gym.

The band showed up twenty minutes early and started playing.

I noticed Jasmine on crutches slowly making her way to the place where the cheerleaders would sit. When she saw me, she glared at me and muttered something.

I thought about going over and talking to her and maybe telling her again I was sorry I'd hurt her when I swung her but decided that would only make her madder. So I went and sat where the team would be sitting.

A minute later Melissa, a girl from the pep band, approached me. "Cameron, you're going to be speaking, aren't you?"

"Who else would do that except me?" I said.

"Can you do me a favor? Do you know Mr. Walters? He's the band director, and he's my uncle. He has to take early retirement and this is his last day, so could you say something nice about him?"

"What would I say?"

"How important the pep band has been at the games."

That made me laugh. "Actually, the pep band isn't that important, at least not to the team."

"Is it going to kill you to say a nice word about Mr. Walters?" she asked.

"Let me think about it, okay?"

She started getting all emotional on me. "You're not going to do it, are you?"

"I didn't say I wouldn't. I just need to think about it, that's all. This rally is for the team. I'm not sure I want to waste time on some pep band director."

Melissa looked like she was about to cry. "Cameron, he's dying of cancer."

"So? Look, tell me when he dies. I'll send a card."

"He's worked his whole life at this school."

"And that's my fault?"

Melissa glared at me and walked away. She returned to the pep band, sat down next to Madison, and started talking. I figured she was telling her what I'd said because Madison glared at me and shook her head.

Coach Grogan entered the gym and came over to talk to me. "So you'll introduce the team, right? Say a few words about the game and the season, then introduce Mrs. Austin. She'll introduce the cheerleaders. They'll lead us in a cheer. Then introduce me. After I speak, we'll sing the school song. Any questions?"

"No, I got it."

"Oh, one other thing. It's Mr. Walters' last day. He's the band director. Could you say a couple of nice things about him and the band?"

"Why can't *you* do that?" I grumbled.

"It'll mean more coming from a student. Just say something."

I sighed. "Yeah, okay, I guess."

"Oh, one more thing. I've spent the last half hour on the phone, talking to the coach of USC. He's really interested in you."

"Are you serious? That's great!"

"I gave him your home number. He's going to call you tonight, so stay home until he calls."

"You can count on that! Man, this is like a dream come true!"

The pep rally was everything I wanted it to be. I enjoyed introducing every member of the team and talking about our season. "Every game was tough, especially after we'd won five games in a row. After that, every team was out to get us, but that only made us work harder. I can't say enough about these guys. It's easy to look good with an offensive line like we had that opened up holes you could drive a truck through."

Five minutes later I was still talking. Coach got my attention and pointed at his watch.

"I've got to wrap this up. Let's have Mrs. Austin come up here and introduce the cheerleaders. What would we do without the cheerleaders? I know they always cheer me up!" I started laughing. "Every last one of them!"

By then everyone in school knew about the bet I'd made so that got a big laugh from the guys. Not so much from the girls, though.

Apparently Mrs. Austin had also heard about me and the cheerleaders. As she took the mic, she placed her hand over it and muttered, "You stay away from my girls."

She was scary, so I backed away and sat down.

I could tell she was still mad at me as she talked about how dedicated the cheerleaders were and how much they had practiced and how they helped foster school spirit. She introduced each of the cheerleaders who then did a couple of cheers.

And then I took over again. "One more thing before I turn it over to the coach. Mr. Walters, would you please stand up? This is Mr. Walters' last day. Mr. Walters, we'd like to thank you and the pep band for filling up the slack time during our games. Good luck to you."

The band stood up and cheered, then played a song in tribute to Mr. Walters. I resented them taking up so much time. As soon as they finished, I announced, "Whatever. Give it up for the most successful coach in the state! Coach Grogan!"

Everyone stood, yelling and applauding.

Coach Grogan praised the team and talked about our season. Just before finishing, he officially presented me the game ball. After the rally was over, the team and I stayed around to visit with anyone who wanted to talk with us.

Thirty minutes later, in the hall, as I approached my locker, I saw Toby waiting for me.

"You again?" I asked. "You want me to put you in the locker again? If I do it this time, I swear I'll leave you in there overnight."

Toby had this weird look on his face, and he quickly pulled a gun from his jacket pocket and pointed it at me. "I want you to take back all the lies you've been telling about Emma Jean," he yelled.

He was such a wimp, it didn't even scare me. "Come on, Toby, don't do something stupid. I never said anything bad about Emma Jean."

"You must have said something."

"Ask anyone on the team. They'll tell you."

Some students, seeing the gun, hurried for the exits, but others stayed around to see what was going to happen.

"What are people saying about me and Emma Jean?" I asked.

"They're saying that you and she . . ." Toby couldn't do it.

"You'll have to tell me or I won't know what you're talking about."

Toby was near tears. He gestured with the gun. "You know what they're saying! Tell everyone the truth about what happened or I'll shoot you."

I didn't want to admit I was responsible for the rumors about Emma Jean, but I also did not want to be shot. So what was I going to do?

It was then I realized I still had the game ball in my hand. "Okay, Toby, you win. I'll tell everyone the truth."

"Say it loud enough so that everyone can hear."

Mr. Jacobson, a science teacher, was on the perimeter of the crowd and moved through the students toward Toby, trying to get students to leave the school.

I turned to the crowd. "Okay, everyone, listen up! Can you all hear me? If you can hear me, raise your hands."

As Toby turned to glance at the upraised hands, I threw the football as hard as I could. It hit Toby in the face, knocking him down. As he fell, the gun went off, firing a shot into the ceiling.

"Go! Go! Go!" the teacher yelled to the students, who began running toward the exits.

Toby sat up and slowly turned the gun toward himself.

"No!" I yelled. I dove, grabbing Toby's wrist and twisting the gun out of his hand. "What are you doing? Are you crazy?"

Toby didn't answer. He just sat there staring at the floor.

The principal arrived and sat down next to Toby and put his arm around his shoulders, I guess making sure he didn't do anything else stupid.

A few minutes later a dozen policemen charged into the school. They pushed Toby onto his face and handcuffed his hands behind his back and then hauled him out of the school. Then they asked me some questions about what had happened and congratulated me on taking charge of the situation. Then they left.

"What's going to happen to him?" I asked the principal.

"They'll probably send him to a juvenile detention facility. I'm just glad you were able to disarm him."

"Always glad to help out. Just one question."

"What's that?" he asked.

"Do you think I should wait for the media to come and interview me about my quick response here that saved who knows how many lives or should I just go home?"

He seemed annoyed by the question. "Just go home, Cameron. You've done enough for one day. Just go home."

"Good idea."

"I take it from what Toby said that there are some rumors going around about you and his sister, Emma Jean."

"Who knows? The guy's totally delusional."

"So you had no part in this?"

"None at all."

"How did the rumors get started?"

I shrugged. "Who knows how rumors ever get started? Well, I've got to go. Hey, guess what? I might get to play for USC. Their coach is going to call me at home tonight."

"That's great, Cameron. Looks like everything is going your way."

"Looks that way. Well, I've got to go. See you tomorrow."

I made my way toward the front of the school. The halls were empty now, and I noticed an unusual glow in the breeze-way behind the two sets of doors leading outside.

As I went through the first door, the light became brighter, and I was having a hard time making my way to the second door. I felt like I was running in mud or swimming upstream in a big river.

My outstretched hand was within a few inches of the outside door when the door behind me opened by itself and a blast of air hit me in the chest and blew me back into the school.

"Great game, Cameron!" the same guy as from the morning called out.

I stopped and looked around. Everything was the way it had been earlier that morning.

"What's going on?"

I turned around to leave the school again, went through the first set of doors on my way out of the building, when the light and the whooshing sound started in again, blasting me back into the school.

"Great game, Cameron!"

"Quit saying that!"

"What's your problem?"

"Never mind," I said. "Come here. I want you to hold this door open so I can get a run at the second door. Okay?"

"I guess so," the guy said.

"What's your name?" I asked.

"Andy."

I backed halfway down the hall, stopped, and yelled to Andy, "Tell me when there's nobody coming into the building, so I don't hit them on my way out."

He glanced at the front door. "Now is a good time," he said.

I took off running as fast as I could, breezed past Andy who was holding the door open, and came within an inch of my finger touching the outer door when a tornado-force wind caught me and blew me back into the school again.

"Great game, Cameron!" Andy said.

"Is this some kind of a joke? What day is it?"

"It's Monday. Today is the pep rally."

Shaking my head, I slowly made my way down the hall to my locker.

Somehow it was Monday morning.

Again.

CHAPTER TWO

s I approached my locker, Madison was waiting for me.
"You again?" I grumbled, glaring at her. "You're like a
horrible nightmare that keeps coming back again and again."

She pursed her lips. "I am?"

Out of habit I opened my locker and then turned to face her.
"Let me guess, you're here to interview me for the stupid school
paper, right?"

"Right. Can you talk to me now?"

"I have nothing to say. All I want is to get out of this place."

"Will you be at the pep rally?" she asked.

"You think I care about some stupid rally?" I slammed my locker
door shut. "You know what? There's more than one way out of
here!" I pushed past her and started down the hall. She had to walk
fast to keep up with me. "How about if I tag along and ask a couple
of questions?"

"I don't care what you do."

"I'll try not to take too much of your time."

We ended up near the seldom-used back entrance of the school.

Most people used the front entrance because it was closer to the parking lot.

She looked at her notes. "For you personally, what was it like to win the state football title?"

"It's how we did it that's important," I mumbled, repeating back what I'd said before. But then I panicked. "Do you want to know what scares me the most? The thought of not having a future. You take having a future for granted, don't you? So did I, until now. But, you know what? I'm not going to give up."

She looked confused. "What do you mean about not having a future?"

I shook my head. "Later, okay?" I ran as fast as I could toward the door. Another flash of light was followed by the same strong wind.

A second later I found myself back inside the school again.

Maybe I made it this time, I thought because Andy wasn't there to greet me.

Then a locker door slammed next to me and Andy stepped away from his locker. "Great game, Cameron!"

It was early Monday morning, again.

"I'm not giving up, you hear me!" I yelled, hurrying toward my locker.

"That's the spirit! Like you never gave up at the game, right?" Andy called out after me.

Madison was there, waiting for me. "Have you seen the custodian?" I asked.

"Yeah, he stepped into the boys' restroom a minute ago with a mop."

"I've got to talk to him."

"Can we do a follow-up interview now?" she asked.

"Quit pestering me, okay?"

"I just need five minutes."

I spotted the custodian coming out of the men's room. "When are you going to empty the trash into the dumpster?" I asked.

"As soon as I get the leak stopped in the restroom. Why? Did you lose something?"

"Yeah," I said with a sigh. "I've lost . . . well . . . Tuesday."

He nodded. "You might check lost and found."

Madison followed me as I hurried to the dock where the night custodian left the trash cans. "What thoughts are going through your mind after winning the state title?" she asked.

"My mom got me a new bed about a month ago. It's one of those beds where you dial the comfort number you want. What if I never get to sleep in it again?"

She seemed confused. "Actually, I don't think this is the slant we're looking for, you know, in this story."

I pulled out a full trash bag and shoved it into another container. At the bottom of the now empty container I found a new trash bag. I stood on a chair and, with a little help from Madison, slowly lowered myself into the now empty trash container. I then stepped into the new garbage bag and pulled it up around me.

I knelt down. "Tie this up for me, but not too tight or I won't be able to breathe."

"I know this is none of my business, but why are you doing this?"

"Just tie it up, okay?"

"If you say so." She tied the bag. "There."

"Great. That's it. You can go now," I said.

A few seconds passed but I hadn't heard her leave.

"Are you still there?" I asked.

She didn't answer.

"Are you there or not?"

"Sorry. I saw some of my friends down the hall, and I didn't want them, you know, to see me talking to a, well . . . a trash container. Can you tell me why you're doing this? I promise I won't put it in the paper. I'm just curious."

"I want the custodian to think I'm a useless pile of garbage."

"So . . . uh . . . you're having . . . self-esteem issues?"

"Look, would you just get out of here?" I shot back.

"All right, I'm going. Be careful, though."

I heard her walk away.

There wasn't enough room for me to sit down, so after a while my legs were killing me because of having to squat.

A few minutes later, though, I heard the trash container next to me being rolled across the floor. The door to the dock slammed shut as the custodian rolled the trash container outside.

My container was the next one to go.

"Man, this is heavy," the custodian complained to himself as he tilted the container I was in and began to roll it toward the door.

As the trash container moved closer to the door, I noticed a small light appearing inside the trash bag.

Suddenly the light became much brighter, and I could hear the whooshing sound again. I ripped the trash bag open and stood up. "No!" I shouted, giving the custodian the shock of his life.

A second later I was blown back into the school through the usual entrance.

"Great game, Cameron!"

Once again, Madison was waiting for me at my locker.

"Can we do a follow-up interview now?" she asked. "I know you'll be busy later on. Especially with the victory rally this afternoon."

This was driving me crazy. "I've tried every door! But you know what? I am getting out of here this morning, one way or the other!"

She managed to keep up with me with me as I hurried down the hall. "You seem a little distracted," she said. "Could you just answer this one question? For you, personally, what was it like to win the state football title?"

I stopped walking and looked into a class in progress on the first floor. "I've got it! I know a way out of here!"

I ran into the classroom to the row of chairs next to the window.

"You can't come barging into my classroom!" the teacher complained.

I glared at a timid-looking geek. "Get out of your chair! I need it."

The guy, intimidated by me, stood up and backed away.

I picked up the chair, threw it through the window, and then stood up on the window ledge.

"Stop him!" the teacher called out.

I jumped.

But just before my feet would have left the window ledge, I heard the whooshing sound and saw the light. And suddenly I was blasted back into the school through my usual entrance.

"Great game, Cameron!" Andy called out.

I'd had it! I stormed to my locker where Madison was waiting. Before she could say anything, I asked, "Do you remember me crawling into a dumpster and climbing into a trash bag and then you tying up the bag?"

She looked confused. "No. When did this happen?"

"Today," I said with a deep sigh. "Everything happens today. I don't suppose you remember me trying to jump out the window, either, do you?"

"What? You must have me confused with some other girl. Remember when I interviewed you last week? I'm supposed to do a follow-up interview with you. Just a couple of questions. Can you do it now?"

I shrugged my shoulders. "Why not? I have nothing else to do for the rest of my life."

"If you want, we could go in the library to talk. It'll be quieter there." She paused. "That is, unless you would, you know, feel more comfortable . . . uh . . . you know . . . in a dumpster."

"The library's okay," I grumped.

As we sat down across from each other at a table, I propped my elbows on the table and rested my head in my hands. "I don't know what to do. I've tried everything, but nothing works."

"What do you need to do? Can I help?"

I shook my head. "Nobody can help me."

"When I'm having a bad day, I call my mom and talk to her."

I sat up. "Great idea! I'll call my mom, and she'll come and get me."

I grabbed my cell phone and punched in the numbers. A voice came on the line and said, "Your service has been interrupted. Call again later."

I turned to her. "My cell isn't working. Can I try yours?"

"Yeah, sure." She handed me hers. I got the same message.

She called her mom and got through. "Oh, nothing, just seeing how you were."

When I tried the library phone, it was dead.

I kept trying but continued to hear that my service was interrupted and that I needed to call later.

"Do you want to tell me what your problem is?" Madison asked.

"I want to leave school but I can't."

"Why drop out now? It's only a few more months until we graduate."

I shook my head. "You know what? It's totally useless to talk to you about this."

"Just tell me what the problem is," she said.

"It's so weird. Every time I try to leave the school, I get whooshed back in, and it's always Monday morning. And there's a bright light that comes with the wind."

She winced. "Well I'm sure that happens . . . you know . . ." She cleared her throat. ". . . to a lot of people."

"You think I'm out of my mind, don't you?"

"No, no, not at all. Not exactly. You're just . . . uh . . . well . . . confused." She shook her head. "I'm sorry. I'm not very good at this. But at least let me say this—I'm here for you."

"Yes, you are. Every stupid day you're waiting for me outside my stupid locker."

She shook her head. "Just today."

"That's right, just today. But, don't you see, it's always today. Today never ends."

"This day never ends?"

"Isn't that what I just said?"

She took a clump of her hair and nervously began to twist it. "Have you seen the school nurse about this? She might have some pills, you know, to help you, uh, calm down."

"She'd think I was crazy."

"The word *crazy* is such an unkind way of describing people who are . . . well . . ." She stopped and sighed.

"Delusional? Psycho?" I suggested. "Go ahead, pick one. You think I don't know how this must sound to you?" I stood up and began pacing back and forth. "I've tried every door. I tried jumping out of a window. I even tried to hide in a trash bag. You helped by tying up the bag."

Confused, she stuck the ends of the twisted hair into her mouth. "When did all this happen?" she asked.

"It happens every time I try to leave the stupid school."

Once she realized what she was doing with her hair, she stopped and started going through her backpack. "You know what? I've got some Tylenol in here somewhere."

"I don't need anything."

"Not for you. For me," she said. She found the Tylenol bottle and shook out two pills. "I need some water to get these down. I'll be back in a minute."

By the time she returned, I'd had an idea. "Maybe if I don't try to leave, like if I stay here all night, then in the morning it would be Tuesday, right?"

"That makes sense to me. Even here at school, Monday eventually turns . . . you know . . . into Tuesday." She furrowed her eyebrows and looked at me as though I were completely crazy.

"Would you stay here with me tonight and keep me company?" I asked.

She cleared her throat. "Uh, I'm pretty sure my folks wouldn't approve of me spending the night with you, even in an educational setting such as this." She stood up. "But you know what? I hope everything works out for you. I've got to go now. Nice talking to you."

"I hope I never see you again."

She took it personally. "You do?"

"I didn't mean it the way it sounded. Thanks for being such a caring person."

"I hope it helped. Well, 'bye."

I watched her leave. *She seems like a good person*, I thought.

Relieved that now, at least, I had a plan, I decided to go to all my classes.

This time, during first period, I didn't spread any rumors about Emma Jean.

In my eleven o'clock class, I finished Mrs. Arnold's test, found out what questions I'd missed, whooshed myself back to Monday, and after talking to Madison again, took the test again. I was finished in ten minutes.

"That didn't take very long," Mrs. Arnold said.

"Could you grade it? I want to see what I got on it."

As she began grading, her red pencil was eagerly poised to put a big X on the questions I missed. When she finished, she seemed disappointed that I'd done so well. "You got them all right," she said, sounding amazed.

"I think I'll get A's on all my tests from here on in," I said.

She looked at me and shook her head as though she were puzzled. "Well, I hope you do, Cameron."

At the rally I spotted Madison in the pep band. When I gave my talk about our season, I tried not to sound like a conceited jerk. She seemed to be okay with that approach. And I was a little kinder to Mr. Walters than the first time I'd done it, telling him how much he had meant to the school and wishing him well in his battle with his illness.

After school, since I planned to stay the night there, I kept one step ahead of the night custodian until he went home. Then I loaded up on food from the vending machine, went to the room where they stored the wrestling mats, and settled in for the night.

After downing two or three snacks and a couple of cans of soda, it was hard to get to sleep, but eventually I did. Except, I kept having the strangest dream. In my dream I was lying on my back and it was night and I couldn't move, and there was this girl, maybe a witch or some creature from another world, and she was standing over me, and she had a silver-like wand in her hand. I was certain that she was going to cast an evil spell over me. I desperately wanted to get away, but for some reason I couldn't move. I know it sounds stupid, but I was terrified of her.

When I woke up the next morning, it was a brand new day.

"I did it! I made it to Tuesday! I'm home free."

The halls were empty at that early hour as I walked down the hall toward the door leading out of the school. As I got closer to an outside door, that same bright light I had seen almost blinded me, and a wind started to push me toward the outer doors.

"No!!! Not again!"

The students who were now filling the halls didn't seem to even see me as I slid past them, picking up speed.

"Somebody help me!" I shouted. I grabbed a classroom door and hung onto it. But a strong blast of wind yanked me away and I continued sliding faster and faster through the first outer door, and then thrown back into the school again.

"Great game, Cameron!"

I went over to Andy and shouted at him. "I will get out of here, one way or the other! You hear me, one way or the other!"

He kind of stepped back, as though he were afraid of me, and muttered, "Hey, Cameron. It's me, Andy. What's up? Are you okay?"

I spent the rest of the morning dodging Madison and making preparations for an even more desperate attempt to escape. A little past noon, with the cafeteria crowded with students eating lunch, I entered waving what appeared to be a gun. "All right, this is a stickup! Everybody get on the floor!"

I approached the girl at the cash register. "Give me everything you've got!"

"Hi, Cameron! Great game! Okay, well, the thing is, mostly I check names off this list. But if you want, I can give you the list."

"I know you've got money in there! Give it to me!"

She opened the drawer and grabbed a few dollar bills and some quarters.

"You want the pennies, too?"

"No." I grabbed the dollar bills and waved them in front of everyone. "You see this? I'm robbing the cafeteria with a gun! That's armed robbery. Anyone got a problem with that?"

Madison entered the cafeteria, spotted me, and walked over to me. "I've been looking all over for you. I need to do a follow-up interview with you for the school paper."

"Can't you see I'm busy here?"

"What are you doing?"

"I'm robbing the cafeteria!"

She laughed. "Yeah, right."

I pointed the gun at her. "Don't make me use this on you!"

She leaned closer to examine the gun then reached over and bent the barrel. "You made this out of modeling clay, didn't you?"

"Go away! I'm robbing the cafeteria, and if you don't like it, why don't you use your cell phone and call the cops?"

"No problem." She took out her cell phone, glanced at me, and punched in the numbers. "Yes, I'd like to report an armed robbery at the high school cafeteria."

After answering all the 911 operator's questions, she put her cell phone back in her backpack. "You'd better leave now because the police are coming."

"I'm not going anywhere. I'm staying here until they arrest me."

"And then what?"

"They'll take me away from here and book me for armed robbery. But you know what? Anything will be better than staying here for the rest of my life."

A guy came up to me. "Cameron, is it okay if I use the restroom?"

"Hey, I'm doing an armed robbery here, okay? Wait until I get arrested."

"I need to leave, too, Cameron," a girl pleaded. "But if you want, I'll come right back."

"Yeah, like I believe that."

"I'd come back for you, Cameron," the girl said. "Especially after the great job you did as a quarterback for our team this year."

"We all feel the same way," the boy who needed to use the restroom agreed.

My shoulders sagged. "Look, I'm sorry if I scared any of you guys. And let me say we really appreciated your support this season. You guys are the greatest."

From behind a wall, a police officer called out, "We've got you surrounded! Put down your weapon and come out with your hands up."

"Sorry for the scare," I called out to everyone.

I set the modeling clay gun on the floor and stepped away from it. With my hands up, I walked slowly toward the policeman. "I surrender."

The police officer ordered me to lie down and put my arms behind me. He quickly handcuffed me, and the place was suddenly flooded with cops. They helped me get into a standing position, and two officers led me toward the outside door.

"Could you handcuff me to each of you?" I asked.

"Why would we do that?"

"Sometimes I have trouble leaving school."

"You won't have trouble today. Take a good look. You'll never be back here again."

"You have no idea how good that sounds to me! Would you guys mind if we ran toward the door to build up some momentum?"

"Yes, we would mind."

Once they were through the first door, the sound and the light began building all over again.

"Push me through!" I shouted to the two police officers.

As we got closer to the door, the force against us increased. And then they disappeared, and I was once again standing alone in the hall of the school. And it was Monday morning again.

"No!" I shouted.

I raised my arms into the air. "All right, if this is the game I must play, then I will play it to win! No more Mister Nice Guy!"

"Great game, Cameron!"

I shoved Andy into the wall of lockers. "Get out of my way, you stupid idiot!"

CHAPTER THREE

fter being caught three times walking off with a tray of freshly baked cookies in the kitchen of the school cafeteria, I finally managed to time it just right.

I ate the entire tray of cookies. They made me a little sick so I just made another attempt to leave the school. When I was pushed back to Monday morning again, it was as if I hadn't eaten anything.

The next time I stole the cookies, I decided to share some of them with Madison. Of course I found her in front of my locker. "Madison, want a cookie?"

"Can we do a follow-interview now?" she asked. "I know you'll be busy later on. Especially with the victory rally this afternoon."

"If you take a cookie, I'll do it."

She took a cookie from the tray.

"Let's go into the library," I suggested.

We found a secluded table in a far corner of the room. "Go ahead with your questions," I said.

She looked at her notes. "For you, personally, what was it like to win the state football title?"

I stacked five cookies on top of each other and took a big bite. "Sorry," I said, still chewing. "To answer your question, it was great winning state."

"Do you have anything to add to that?"

"Not really." I shoved the rest of the five cookies into my mouth.

"Why are you doing that?" she asked.

"I've found a way to eat anything I want and never gain weight or get sick or anything. I could eat a hundred cookies a day and never gain a pound."

"Are you bulimic?" she asked.

"No, I just have a really fast metabolism. You want to know how fast? Two seconds and it's all taken care of."

"If all it takes is two seconds, you are bulimic."

I grabbed six cookies, molded them into a ball, and then took a bite.

"Is that all you're going to do today?" she asked. "Eat cookies?"

"Yeah, pretty much."

"If all you think about is your stomach, you're wasting your life."

"What else is there to think about?" I asked.

"Life isn't just about ourselves. We're here on this earth to serve others."

I laughed. "That is so naive! We're here to take what we can get. And if someone gets in the way, then that's too bad for them."

"Do you care about anyone in this school besides yourself?" she asked.

I took another big bite. "Not really. Should I?"

"You could help people, Cameron."

"Why would I want to do that?"

That made her mad. "You're right. I can't think of any reason why you would want to help anyone. You just keep stuffing those stupid cookies into your mouth. That's where you'll find true joy and happiness."

I wiped my mouth with my sleeve. "I'm glad you see it my way. Excuse me. I'm going to get some more cookies."

"Have you ever noticed there are actually other people in this school besides yourself? Do you ever wonder if any of them have problems? Or are you too caught up in the wonder of yourself? Just a word or two from you could make a difference in their lives if only you could get your mind off yourself once in a while."

I looked at her as if I were taking her message to heart and then grinned. "You were trying to make me feel guilty, weren't you? Too bad it didn't work. Excuse me. Time for more cookies."

The next time I stole a tray of cookies, I took them to the varsity locker room to share with the team.

"So, who was that girl you were with Saturday night after the cheerleaders bailed?" Wade asked.

"Emma Jean."

"What did you two do after the rest of us left?"

"Nothing."

"Yeah, right," Wade said. "Like we believe that. The way I hear it, you were with her all night."

"Sorry to disappoint you, but we both fell asleep. Nothing happened."

"C'mon, Cameron. It's not like you to hold anything back from us."

"There's nothing to tell."

"Make something up then."

"No." I paused. "I've already done that and I nearly got killed for it."

As the talk switched to another topic, I wondered if the reason I'd refused to spread rumors about Emma Jean was because I knew what Madison would think of me if I did that. I hoped that wasn't the case. I was not about to let some girl change the way I thought or what I did.

A few minutes before my eleven o'clock class, the guy who sat next to me asked if I'd studied for the test.

"I don't need to. I know all the questions on the exam and the answers."

"How about sharing with your friends?"

"Sure, no problem." I grabbed a piece of paper and wrote out the answers to the questions, then handed it over.

"Thanks."

"Always glad to help out."

"You mind if I share it with Jessica?"

"No, go ahead, share it with anyone you want."

"You're the greatest."

"It's true. I am."

A few people in the class refused to cheat but almost everyone else did. Those who did were grateful to me for helping them out.

On my way to lunch, a girl approached me. "I understand you had the answers to Mrs. Arnold's test. I have a math test at two o'clock. Is there any chance you could get the answers to that for me?"

"What would you give me for that?" I asked.

"A big hug."

I smiled. "How about a hug and two dollars?"

It took me over thirty transitions back to Monday, but by talking to students as they were leaving a test, I was able to get the answers to all the tests given that day in school.

The next Monday I had a great business selling the answers. Two dollars for a multiple choice test, three dollars for answers to essay questions.

I set up a table outside the cafeteria, ran off a few flyers for some bogus cause, and began selling answers to any student who had heard about my little operation.

And that's where Madison found me. "Can we do a follow-up interview now?" she asked. "I know you'll be busy later on. Especially with the victory rally this afternoon." She pulled out her notebook to write on.

"This is a big day for you, isn't it?"

"You got any tests today?" I asked her.

"Yes, why?"

"I'll sell you the key to the test for a dollar. That's half off the regular price."

"No thanks."

"It's an automatic A for you."

"I'd rather earn my grade instead of buying it."

"Really? Well, it's up to you."

She looked at her notes. "For you, personally, what was it like to win the state football title?"

"Let me ask you a question. Why do you dress the way you do? You're not that bad-looking, actually. If you dressed more like other girls, you'd have a lot more guys like me paying attention to you."

She laughed. "Thanks for the warning."

"Does it bother you at all that you're totally ignored by guys like me?"

"No, actually, it's a relief."

"I tell you what I'll do. What class is your test in?"

"Mr. McPherson's biology class."

"Just a minute." I shuffled through a stack of papers until I found the answers to Mr. McPherson's test. I handed it to her. "No charge. Have a nice day."

"No thanks," she said, refusing to take the sheet from me.

"Everyone else in the class will get an A except for you."

"That doesn't matter. I'm here to learn."

"Yeah, me too. You want to know what I've learned so far? How to game the system. And that's what I'm doing now."

"How about if I just make up a quote from you about the football game?"

"Yeah, you do that, Twinkle Toes."

I made twenty dollars selling answers to tests given that day. The only problem was the next time I began another Monday the money was gone. So I gave up on that idea.

The next time I started out another variation of Monday, I decided to track down Emma Jean, thinking I could use her to make life a little more interesting. I found her walking to class with a couple of weird girls. I stopped her and told her two friends to get lost. Then I said to her, "Emma Jean, I just want you to know I've been thinking about you night and day since Saturday night."

The way she smiled, I could tell she was a girl who had never had anyone say that to her. "You have?" she asked.

"Absolutely. So I was wondering if we could see each other on a regular basis."

"Are you saying that you want me to be your girlfriend?"

"Exactly. Maybe you could come with me to whatever college I play football for. And then if that works out, we'll get married."

"I'm only a junior."

"No problem. I'll play for a couple of years and then we'll get married."

She looked nervous and confused. "I . . . uh, I don't know what to say."

"I know. It's sudden. Do you believe in love at first sight, Emma Jean?"

She nodded her head enthusiastically. "I do! I always have!"

"Me too. For sure," I said.

"I can hardly wait to tell Toby."

"Absolutely. How about tonight I come over to your place and we tell both your mom and dad and Toby?"

"Sure, that'd be great." She paused. "Except my dad doesn't live with us anymore. He skipped off with some woman about a year ago."

"Things like that happen."

"It's been the hardest on Toby. He doesn't say much about it, though, but I can tell he's hurting."

"Look, this is so great to talk to you, and, for sure, I'll come over tonight and meet your mom and Toby, but for right now, I'd really like to spend some time alone with you, like we did Saturday night, uh, talking."

"Where?"

"I know a place in school where we can be alone. I think it's so important for couples to talk, don't you?"

I led her down the hall heading for the mat room.

Madison was standing by her locker and saw us as we walked by. "Cameron, Emma Jean, wait up!"

"Just keep walking," I told Emma Jean.

"Madison is one of my best friends."

Madison caught up to Emma Jean and gave her a hug. "How are you doing?"

"Great!" Emma Jean said.

"Cameron, can we do a follow-up interview now?" Madison asked. "I know you'll be busy later on."

"I'm with Emma Jean. Can't it wait?"

"That's okay," Emma Jean said. "I don't mind. Cameron is going to show me a place where we can talk."

"Where is it, Cameron?" Madison asked, all suspicious.

"Well, it's kind of a storage room."

She gave me knowing look. "I think I'll just tag along with you guys."

After I unlocked the door and let them in the room where the wrestling mats were stored, Madison turned to me and said, "So, Cameron, why have you brought Emma Jean here? You think she's interested in smelly wrestling mats?"

"Cameron just asked me to go with him. If things work out, we're going to get married some day."

"Really?" Madison said. "Emma Jean, how well do you know Cameron?"

"We were together at a party Saturday night."

"So you guys had a chance to talk and get acquainted then, right?"

"Well, we didn't actually talk much," Emma Jean said.

"What *did* you do?" Madison asked.

Madison was making me mad. "Hey, don't you have a class or something?" I asked.

"I do. And I'm late for it. Emma Jean has a class, too. Come on, Emma Jean, let's go. You can talk to Cameron later."

Emma Jean sighed. "She's right, Cameron. I should go to class."

After they left, I was so mad that I started kicking the wrestling mats.

A short time later I decided on a different tactic. I found one of the girl cheerleaders at her locker.

"Melanie, I've been looking all over for you."

"My name is Megan."

I shrugged. "Right. Megan. There's something I need to tell you. On Friday night during the game, when it looked like we might lose, I looked over to you on the sidelines, and I'm like, 'You know what? Melanie . . . sorry . . . Megan believes we can win. So maybe we can.' So I just wanted you to know that you inspired me to keep trying and not give up."

She seemed surprised and delighted. "Seriously?"

"Without a doubt."

"That is so great!"

"Since then, I haven't been able to get you out of my mind. You're so . . . uh, athletic. When you and the other cheerleaders shout out, you know, whatever it is you shout out, well, I just want to say, it's so inspiring."

"Wow, thanks! I've wondered if the players even notice."

"Well now you know. Would you mind if I gave you a hug?"

"No, not at all."

I held her in my arms. "This feels so good."

"I don't think Wayne will mind either because this is about cheerleading."

A large farm boy, with hands as big as canned hams, had by then hurried down the hall and was now standing in front of us.

"This is Wayne," Megan said, pulling away from me.

I noticed that Wayne's fists were clenched and his face was red and angry looking.

"Are you messing with my girl?" he challenged.

"No, not at all. I just wanted Melanie to know what an inspiration she was to the team. All of the team, actually."

"It's Megan," she whispered to me.

"Whatever," I muttered.

"Go to class, Megan," Wayne said. "I need to talk to this clown."

"Don't hurt him, Wayne. He's a quarterback."

"Just go."

Megan walked away.

Wayne grabbed me by the shirt and shoved me into the wall. "You know much about FFA?"

"Not really."

"It stands for Future Farmers of America," Wayne said in a low but threatening voice. "It's a club here in school. Most of the guys in FFA weigh close to three hundred pounds. We don't go out for sissy sports like football because when school gets out, we have chores to do. You want to know something else? We're going to be looking for you today. And when we find you, it won't be pretty. We don't like city people hugging our girls." He shoved me into the wall again and stormed away.

I ran to the outside doors and quickly made the transition to the beginning of another Monday so I wouldn't have to worry about FFA guys as big as bulls chasing me.

At lunch I went to a table where a bunch of sophomore girls were sitting. "Hi, girls. I'm looking for someone to make out with for about half an hour."

Six girls raised their hands.

"Actually, I only need one." I said.

"We don't mind."

"All right, let's go then. But let me warn you. I'm shallow and self-centered, and nothing will come of this. I'm never going to contact you again. In fact, I'll probably forget all your names, if I even actually learn them."

"We don't care," one of the girls said, laughing. "We just want to tell everyone we made out with you, Cameron."

"Great, can we go now? I'm kind of in a hurry."

As we left, one of the girls called out to one of her friends. "C'mon! We're all going to make out with Cameron."

"I want to come, too!"

"C'mon, c'mon, I don't have all day," I grumbled.

I looked down the hall before they started, looking for any sign of Madison. The coast was clear.

We all started walking down the hall. "Don't walk with me," I said. "Walk behind me. I don't want somebody seeing us and wondering what we're up to."

We were practically at the place where the wrestling mats were stored when Madison stepped out of a classroom.

"Cameron, wait up. Can we do a follow-up interview now?" she asked. "I know you'll be busy later on. Especially with the victory rally this afternoon." She pulled out her notebook to write on. "This is a big day for you, isn't it?"

"Later, okay? I'm busy now." I said.

"Are all these girls following you?" she asked.

"We're going to make out with Cameron!" one of the girls said.

"All of you?"

"Yes, all of us!" They all started giggling.

Madison walked beside me. "So, Cameron, what's going on?"

"What they said."

"You're going to make out with all of them?"

"Yeah, but only one at a time. What's wrong with that?"

"You can't be serious! You don't even know their names, do you?"

"No."

"That's not right."

"I'll tell you what's not right. Living the same stupid day over and over again."

We reached the storage room, and I opened the door. "Okay, girls, who's first?"

"Me! Pick me!" one of the girls cried out.

"I'll be first," Madison said, stepping in front of them all.

"That's not fair," a girl complained.

"Hey, what can I say? I'm a senior," Madison said. "We get preference in everything."

Madison and I entered the room and she closed the door.

I had a big smile on my face. "Well, things are looking up for me today," I said.

"What is wrong with you? These girls were in junior high a few months ago. Why would you even want to kiss them?"

"I have a new goal in life. To kiss every girl in school before the day is over."

"That's impossible."

"For some people it would be, but not for me."

Outside the door, one of the girls called out. "Are you two making out yet?"

"No, we're just talking," Madison called out.

"I think you and I should kiss just to see how we like it," I said to Madison.

"How can you even think about kissing someone you don't even care about?"

"It's not that hard. In fact, in some ways, it's easier."

"To me a kiss should only come after a guy is my best friend. Somebody I respect and know that he respects me, too. Even somebody I believe I could marry some day."

I laughed. "So what you're saying is you've never been kissed, right?"

"I don't see that's any of your business."

"People can be very idealistic before they've been kissed, but once you start kissing, you start to think of it like a scrimmage. It's good practice and sometimes even a lot of fun, but in the end it doesn't count for anything."

"You are so . . . gross. I could never be like that."

"Why not?"

"Kissing can lead to other things."

"So?"

"I want my husband to be my first."

I laughed. "You're kidding, right?"

"No."

"That's not possible."

"It is."

"No, think about it. For you, getting married could be like five years away."

"So?"

"How can anyone wait that long?"

"You can if you set a goal and if you're with people who feel the same way."

"There's nobody like that in this school."

"That might be true, but it doesn't matter. It's still my goal."

"Then I feel sorry for you," I said.

"And I feel sorry for you," she said.

"Don't feel sorry for me. I'll be getting a lot of action from a lot of girls before I finally settle down and get married."

"And so what will your honeymoon mean to you? Just another episode, right? Except maybe you'll actually remember her name. Oh, wait! Let me give you a hint. Her last name will be the same as yours."

I cringed. "That was harsh. I'll remember all their names."

"Really? And how's having other girls to compare your wife with going to improve your marriage?"

"She'll have had others, too."

"And how is that a better way to start a life together?"

I paused. "Well, maybe it isn't the best way to start a marriage, but the truth is I can't wait."

There was another knock at the door. "Are you guys still talking?" one of the girls asked.

Madison opened the door. "Yes, we are."

"We can't wait any longer."

"Yeah, you should go to class," Madison said. "We're leaving, too, actually."

We watched the other girls walk away. I could tell they were disappointed, and I actually felt sorry for them—knowing what they had missed.

I turned to Madison. "You don't like me, do you?" I asked.

"Not very much. Your values are all fouled up. You know, being a good athlete is not what's most important in life."

"Really? What would you say is most important?"

"To live with integrity and to care about others."

"Hey, I care about people."

"Don't confuse using people with caring about them."

"I don't use people."

"Really? You made a bet with the team that you could kiss all the cheerleaders in a week? You expect me to believe you care about any of them? Face it, you are totally self-centered. You use people."

"And you don't, right?" I asked sarcastically.

"No, I have principles that govern my life. I know what I will do, and I know what I won't do. That's been a great help to me."

"You know what? I don't care what you think about me. I'm still going to live my life my way."

"I'm sure you will. You'll make bad choices. You'll leave a path of ruined lives behind you, and you won't care. You'll be selfish until the day you die." She turned and walked away.

I didn't even go to class. I just sat on a wrestling mat and wished I'd never met Madison.

I also got a few hours of sleep.

After I woke up and while I was walking down the hall, I saw another cheerleader. We stopped to talk. "Are you doing anything now? You want to go some place where we can talk? I know a place."

"Have you forgotten the rally?" she asked.

"Oh, yeah. Actually, I'm not sure I'll even go."

"You've got to go. The main reason we won Friday night is because of you."

"That's true. Okay, I'll go."

We headed toward the gym "Do you think I'm self-centered?" I asked.

She nodded. "Yeah, sure. Everybody does."

We entered the gym.

Coach Grogan came over to me. "So you'll introduce the team, right?"

"Yeah, right."

The coach went over the program with me again.

"Oh, one other thing. It's Mr. Walters' last day. He's the band director, so if you could say a couple of nice things about the pep band and him, that would be great."

"Yeah, right," I mumbled.

"Oh, one more thing. I spent the last half hour on the phone talking to the coach of USC. They're interested in you. I gave him your home phone. He's going to call tonight so stick around home."

As he walked away, I shook my head and thought, *I wish I could go home.*

As I sat with the team and waited for the rally to begin, I noticed Madison enter the gym. She stopped and talked to one person after another, always smiling and laughing. But none of them were people I knew. Which meant they were losers.

She also made a point to go and talk with Emma Jean and Toby before she took her place in the pep band.

A few minutes later I was standing at the mic. I felt this sudden rage. I was trapped in this stupid situation and nothing I had done had made any difference. I looked around at the gym full of students, at my team members, and all the teachers. They all looked so happy, I couldn't take it anymore.

"Last year when I sat on the bench almost the whole season just so the coach's son could play, the team did squat. This year, we had the same team except I was the quarterback, and we won state. You make your own conclusions, but it's obvious to me that a big share of our success this year belongs to me."

The place was silent.

"And, Madison, just because I said that does not mean I'm self-centered and conceited, like you think I am. I'm just stating the truth. A team depends on its quarterback. Everybody knows that. This year we had the best in the state. But enough of that. I'm supposed to introduce the team to you."

The team stood up and walked up to where I was standing.

This time for some reason, I couldn't remember the name of the first person in line.

"Are you even on the team?" I asked.

The students laughed.

For my benefit, the coach called out, "Evan Chatterly."

"Evan Hatterly."

"Chatterly," the coach corrected.

"Yeah, whatever. Go back to your seat, Evan."

The next person in line was Gonzales.

"You may not know Gonzales because he's from Mexico. Are you even legal, Gonzales? Maybe that's how he learned to run so fast. Just kidding. If you ever want to meet his family, you can see them every day working in the fields. Okay, Gonzales, sit down."

Gonzales, his face red, stormed out of the gym. Some students began booing me.

The coach approached me. "Sit down, Cameron. I'll introduce the rest of the team."

"I'm not done yet."

"Go sit down!"

"Yeah, sure, but first I need to talk about Mr. Walters."

The coach nodded and stepped back.

I spoke into the mic. "This is Mr. Walters' last day. Can you believe he's been here twenty-five years? What a wasted life, right? I mean, c'mon, who ever pays any attention to the pep band? You think people care, Mr. Walters? Well they don't. Oh, sure, we're supposed to say something nice about you because you got cancer, right? Like anyone cares. Like anyone cares about anything. Life is always the same, and then you die. You know what? I wish I could die. Any change would be good. But no, I'm stuck here with all you losers."

"I said sit down!" the coach roared, reaching for the mic. "You've said enough."

I kept the mic and moved away from him. "Wait, I haven't introduced the cheerleaders. I want everyone to know that I made a bet with the team that I could kiss them all in one week. And I did. Actually, I think any guy in school could do the same thing. Guys, just tell 'em they look great."

"Shut your mouth and sit down!" the coach yelled at me.

I threw the mic on the floor and sat down.

The coach tried to make things better, but the rally was soon over. Nobody said a word to me as the students left, and in a short time I was standing alone in the gym.

I followed Madison to her locker.

"So what did you think?"

"You don't want to know what I think!"

"No, I do."

"You live in a very small world, don't you?"

I was surprised she'd say that to someone who was compelled to live the same day over and over again in one place. I followed her as she headed for the door. "In what way did you mean that?"

"You think you're the star of the show and everyone else is just part of the supporting cast, don't you? The way you see it, the only reason for people like me to exist is to make you look good. Or to cater to your every wish. You need to grow up. That's what I think."

She turned and walked away.

I caught up with her and walked beside her. "Who do you think you are to talk to me that way? I deserve respect. I brought the state football title to this school. And what have you done lately? Nothing. Not a thing. You go to school and nobody who really counts even knows who you are. In five years nobody will even remember you. But they'll always remember me. Any time someone looks at the trophy we brought back from state, they'll remember me."

"Are there other trophies in the trophy case?" she asked.

"Yes there are. Going back twenty years."

"Who won all those trophies? Give me any of their names."

We were at the door. She stopped to let me answer her question.

"I don't know their names," I said.

"In a few years nobody will know your name, either. Or care what you did on the football field."

I felt as though she was telling me the truth, and I hated her for it.

She continued. "But, actually, I'm wrong. You will be remembered. Jorge Gonzales will remember you for insulting him and his family. Mr. Walters and all his family will forever remember your mean-spirited comments on his last day here. The cheerleaders will remember you for disrespecting them. Your team members will remember you taking all the glory for a successful season. Oh, yes, you will be remembered. Good-bye."

She started for the door.

"Don't go. Please don't go."

"Why should I stay?"

"I'm all alone here."

"Yes, you are. And you deserve to be."

And with that she left me.

All alone.

Just me.

And my regrets.

Chapter Four

stayed in the gym until a security guard came and told me I'd have to leave. He escorted me to the door, and as I tried to leave, the same thing happened. I ended up back in the school, starting out another desolate Monday morning.

Andy called out. "Nice game, Cameron." I didn't go to my locker. I went instead to the cafeteria kitchen and stole a butcher knife. I was thinking about killing myself that morning. My options were to stab myself or jump from the second-floor landing.

My only worry was that it wouldn't work. *What if I jump from here and I don't die? And they get me out of the building but then I spend the rest of my life in a wheelchair? I want out of this nightmare, not a worse version of it.*

A school bus pulled up and stopped to let students out. I noticed Emma Jean and Toby getting off the bus with their plastic lunch boxes and garage sale clothes.

I never should have allowed rumors about Emma Jean to go through school, I thought. *That must have been real bad for her to know people were talking about her that way. And I shouldn't have dumped pudding on Toby's head and shoved him in a locker. And when he wanted to shoot me, I should have let him.*

Suddenly I stopped. *Wait a minute. That didn't really happen. Or at least it didn't happen today. Nothing's happened today so far. There's no reason for me to feel bad about something that didn't really happen.*

I wondered why Emma Jean went to the party Saturday night. What was she hoping would happen? True love? Yeah, right. That doesn't even exist.

And what about Toby? Why did he try to kill himself after I hit him with the football in the hall? Maybe because of his dad leaving. I'm the only one who knows he's thinking about killing himself, but who do I tell, and what do I say?

Emma Jean will fall for the first guy who pays any attention to her. What if he's abusive? She'll just assume it's her fault for making him mad. And so her life and that of her kids will be a disaster.

Maybe Toby will silently brood for years and then one day he'll suddenly snap and either hurt himself or someone else.

And then there's Gonzales. What happens to him now? If he'd caught the touchdown pass, his future could be much brighter. I insulted him in front of the whole school. Him and his family. But that wasn't today, either. I haven't done anything today, except think about how to end my life.

I was still trying to decide whether to jump or stab myself when I heard someone behind me. I turned around and there was Madison.

I slid the knife into my backpack without her seeing it. "Madison, how's it going today?"

"Okay. Can we do a follow-up interview now?" she asked. "I know you'll be busy later on. Especially with the victory rally this afternoon." She pulled out her notebook to write on. "This is a big day for you, isn't it?"

After I'd answered all her questions, I said, "Now can I ask you a question?"

"I guess so."

"What if all you had was today? What would you do?" I asked.

"You mean like if I knew this was the last day I'd be alive?"

"Not that dramatic, but something like that. What would you do?"

"I don't know. I've never thought about it before."

"I'd really like to know."

"Well, if I had only one day, I'd want to spend it with my family."

"What if for some reason you couldn't leave school?" I asked.

"Can my family come here?"

"No, you can't get in touch with them, so the only people you can interact with are the people here."

She pursed her lips. "I don't know what I'd do." After a long pause, she said, "One thing though, before I died, I'd want to make a difference in someone's life."

"That doesn't make sense. What do you get out of helping someone else?"

"Peace of mind."

"But if you only have today, and that's all you'll ever have, you'd see all your hopes and plans for the future slipping away. No time to make your dreams come true. What does a person do after he or she has lost all hope for a future?"

"Did you ever know Alicia?"

"No."

"She died last year of leukemia. I talked to her right after the doctor told her she didn't have any hope of living more than a few months. At first she took it really hard, but then she came to accept it. When she was able to go to school, and even afterwards when she was stuck at home, she tried to make every day count. She was always sending notes to people, trying to cheer them up."

"Isn't that backwards? Others should have been trying to cheer her up."

"I know. But as she got worse, she seemed to turn outward to others."

"How come I never even knew about Alicia?"

"I don't know. We did a fund raiser for her. We raised almost a thousand dollars for her medical treatment."

"It must have been in the middle of football season. I get so busy then I don't pay much attention to anything." Even as I said it, I realized that I had probably heard about the fund raiser for Alisa. I must have decided I was too busy for something like that. I shook my head. "It's hard to believe we go to the same school, isn't it?"

"I'm not in the popular group like you," she said.

"Let me ask you a question, you believe we're on earth to serve others, right?"

She seemed surprised. "How do you know I believe that?"

"I must have heard you say it in class. Do you really believe that?"

"Yes."

"How did you come up with that? Nobody else in school feels that way."

"My folks have always taught me that."

"Even if it's true, and even if I wanted to help someone, I wouldn't know where to start."

"You start with the people closest to you and then you branch out from there."

I sighed. "I'm not sure I can do that. Is it okay if I talk to you again sometime? I might have a few more questions."

"Yeah, that would be okay." She looked at me with a puzzled expression. "You're not at all like I thought you'd be."

"How am I different?"

"You think about things more."

"Thinking about life is new to me. But anyway, thanks. I feel better now. I'm going to do what you said and start with the people closest to me."

I watched her leave.

It was still first period. I went to the locker room with the team. Once again, team members asked about Emma Jean. I told them that nothing had happened.

Then I sat down next to Gonzales. "Hey, Jorge, can I talk to you?"

"Why?"

"It won't take long. Please."

Gonzales shrugged his shoulders. "Here?"

"No. Let's go in the gym. I'll throw you the ball."

I grabbed a rack of footballs and started to roll it into the gym.

"What are you doing?" Wade asked.

"I'm going to play catch with Gonzales."

"What for? The season's over."

"Just for fun."

It ended up like a practice except we were in school clothes. Gonzales ran different routes. If I got the ball anywhere near him, he caught it.

After a while, we sat down on one of the bleachers. He was breathing hard from running his routes, but he had a big grin on his face and for the first time I noticed how white his teeth were. As we were cooling down, I said, "I should have thrown you the ball Friday night on that last play. You were open, and you should have had the touchdown, not me."

"Why do you say that?" he asked.

"Because for me, it doesn't matter whether I get a football scholarship or not. My folks will help me pay for college. But for you, it could make a big difference. Right?"

"Why would you care what happens to me?"

"You know, in the past I wouldn't have cared about anyone except myself. But I'm trying to change."

"You don't owe me anything."

"I know that."

We began to pick up the footballs scattered around the gym floor. "What are you going to do after you graduate?" I asked.

"Work until I save up enough money and then go to college."

I thought about that. It really could have made a big difference if I had thrown the ball to him and let him score the game-winning touchdown.

I shook my head. "I messed up at the game. I should have thrown you the ball."

"Because you ran instead of passed? That's not a mistake. It's just a game."

"No, I messed up by not throwing you the ball—but also by not getting to know you better."

He looked a little embarrassed, and when the bell rang, he quickly said, "I've got to get to class."

"Yeah, me, too."

Gonzales tossed the last remaining ball to me. "Thanks for talking to me."

"Yeah, sure."

"See you at the rally," he said.

"Right, I'll be there."

I waited until after classes began again and then I walked the halls. On the second floor, I could hear the band practicing. I hurried to the band room, opened the door, and saw Mr. Walters conducting the band in a song they would later play at the rally. I also noticed Madison. She wasn't playing anything, though. She was just handing out music.

I went in the room and walked over to Mr. Walters.

Mr. Walters stopped the band. "Can I help you?"

"You have a phone call downstairs in the office. They sent me up here to get you."

"All right." Mr. Walters turned to Madison. "You rehearse them while I'm gone."

He handed her his baton, and then left.

As soon as he was out of the room, I stood on the wooden riser next to Madison.

"Mr. Walters doesn't have a phone call. I'm here representing the football team. We want to give a special tribute to Mr. Walters at the rally and I'm going to need your help. What can we do to make his last day here special for him?"

Several students had good suggestions.

"We'll need some money," I said. "Can someone pass a plate or something?"

One of the drummers grabbed a cymbal, stuck a dollar bill on it, and passed it to the person next to him.

"One of you will have to buy whatever it is you decide to give him. It's hard for me to leave school today."

Madison got a big smile on her face. "Let's play something special and dedicate it to him."

"Okay, I'll introduce this during the rally. Let's make this a great day for Mr. Walters. Thank you very much. I've got to get out of here before he gets back."

Melissa followed me out of the band room and into the hall. I stopped when she called to me and she stood looking at me with tears in her eyes. Then she threw her arms around my neck and said, "Thanks for wanting to pay tribute to my uncle. It will mean the world to him."

Having her thank me like that felt good. For a moment I didn't know how to respond but ended up softly saying, "Hey, no problem. He deserves anything we can do for all he's done for this school."

Madison watched until Melissa left and then she approached me. "Thanks for doing this. I didn't expect it from you."

"Me, either. I guess I'm learning from your example."

"I'm proud of you."

"Thanks."

I went to my eleven o'clock class and took Mrs. Arnold's test. I finished it in five minutes and then handed it in. "Could you grade it while I wait?" I asked.

She checked my work. "You got them all right."

"Good. I really understood every question this time."

"You can go now."

"Can I talk to you for a minute, Mrs. Arnold?"

"I don't want to disturb those taking the test."

"Could we just talk outside the door?"

We went outside. With everyone in class, the hall was deserted.

"What is it?" she asked.

"Are you okay, Mrs. Arnold?"

"Yes, of course, why do you ask?"

"I don't know. You've seemed worried about something lately. Is everything all right?"

"I don't see that's any of your concern."

"You're right. It isn't. How long have you taught here?"

"Twenty-five years."

"That's a long time."

"It doesn't seem that long to me."

"Is your husband about to retire?"

She didn't answer immediately, but after a moment said, "No, he died about two years ago."

"I didn't even know that. Sorry."

"There's no reason you would know it."

"When will you retire?"

"I was going to retire in May, but—" She stopped, tears brimming in her eyes. She thought for a moment, then said, "It looks as though I'll have to keep working a little longer."

"Why's that?"

"I just need to, that's all."

"Why?"

"Why are you asking me all these questions?"

"You seem very sad lately."

"I can't see any reason why I should share my personal life with you."

"So who else have you talked to about whatever's bothering you?"

"Nobody."

"Did you and Mr. Arnold have children?"

"Yes, two daughters. They're both married now. We have five grandchildren."

"Have you talked to your daughters about why you have to keep working?"

"No."

"Why not?"

"They're busy with their own lives. I don't want to worry them."

"Maybe they could help."

"No, they couldn't. They're strapped for money as it is."

"Is the reason you have to work longer because of money? What changed that would make you work longer?"

"I did a very stupid thing," she blurted out.

"What did you do?"

"I got an email from a man in Nigeria. He told me about a million dollars that belonged to his family. But the government wouldn't let him take it out of the country. He asked if he could deposit the money in my account and then make it available to him after he left the country. In return, he would give me thirty percent." She paused. "He seemed so nice, and so desperate, I agreed to do it for him."

"I don't see how letting someone deposit money in your account could cost you anything."

"I didn't either. A few days later he sent me an email telling me that he needed ten thousand dollars to bribe a government official. He told me that as soon as I did it, I would receive all the money in my account. And so I took some money out of savings and sent it to him."

"The money from Nigeria didn't come though, did it?"

"No, a day passed, and he emailed that one of the bank officials was threatening to go to the government and report him unless he paid him to be quiet."

"How much?"

"Another ten thousand dollars."

"What did you do?"

"I cashed out of my retirement programs and sent him the money." She shook her head. "On Thursday he contacted me again, saying they were sitting in the office ready to forward the money but the bank officer needed an additional ten thousand dollars, and that as soon as I sent it, they would immediately electronically deposit the money in my account. Only a matter of minutes, he said."

"And you did it?"

"Yes, I did. The money didn't come. On Friday he contacted me again asking for another twenty thousand dollars. I told him I would not be sending him any more money. He told me he was sorry to hear that. He said he would try to get the money to me another way and that by Monday I should have the money. And so I waited."

She stared into space. "The money never came. And now I know it won't come. I've depleted my retirement funds completely, and the only way I can think of to build them back up is to keep working for as long as I can."

"I'm sorry it didn't work out."

"I've been such a fool."

"You need to go to the police."

"I'm too embarrassed. It's bad enough to do what I've done, and

I don't think I can stand to hear a policeman tell me how foolish I've been. I'd almost rather just keep quiet and not say anything."

"You've got to fight back, Mrs. Arnold. If you don't, they'll do this to someone else."

"Maybe later, but not now. I'm too depressed to do much of anything." She suddenly looked into my eyes and said, "You won't tell anyone about this, will you?"

"No, I won't. I promise."

"Thank you for listening to me. I feel better now."

I can't do anything to help her, I thought as I walked the halls. *But at least I got her to talk about it.*

At lunch I sat with the team and talked until I saw Emma Jean and Toby sit down with their lunch boxes.

I went over and sat down with them. "Emma Jean and Toby, how's it going?"

Emma Jean looked surprised I was even talking to her.

Toby glanced up, made eye contact, and then looked back down at the food on his plate. "Okay," he said without any enthusiasm.

"Did you get into any trouble for getting in so late?" I asked Emma Jean.

"Not really. I told my mom what you said."

I wondered what Toby was thinking. "Toby, just so you know, nothing happened Saturday night. We fell asleep watching the video of the game."

Toby nodded.

"I didn't know if you'd even talk to me today," she said.

"Why would you think that?"

"You're the most popular guy in school."

"But what good is it? I'm about to graduate but now I realize there's so many people here I don't even know."

"Like me?" she asked.

I ignored her question but said, "Do you know Madison?"

"She's one of my best friends."

"Well, we had a class together last year, but I never talked to her even though she sat right behind me. What an idiot I was. She's worth getting to know, right?"

Emma Jean nodded. "Madison's a great friend to have."

"Toby, tell me about yourself."

"There's nothing to tell," he mumbled.

"What do you like to do?"

"Play video games in my room."

"Toby is really good at video games," Emma Jean said.

"What else do you like to do?"

"Nothing." Toby stood up to leave.

I panicked. *I've got to do more than this. There must be something I can do to get him to open up.*

"I need to go," Toby said.

"Toby, can I ask you a question? Have you ever thought you'd be better off dead?"

"Why are you asking him that?" Emma Jean asked.

"I've got to go," Toby said.

"Wait just a minute," I said. "There's something I need to tell you. It's really important."

Toby sat back down. "What?"

"I know it's been hard on you what with your dad leaving, but you can't shut down and hold it all inside of you. It helps to talk about things like that."

Toby shook his head. "I don't want to talk about it."

"I know. I'm like that too, sometimes. You might consider getting some counseling."

"I don't want counseling."

"I don't blame you. It's not easy to open up."

Emma Jean reached over and touched Toby on the arm. "Toby, is that true? Have you thought about killing yourself?"

He lowered his gaze and nodded.

"You could've come to me," Emma Jean said. "We could have talked."

"You're having a hard time, too. I didn't want to add to that."

"Toby, I'm your sister. I love you. I want to know how you're doing."

Toby fought back his tears. "It's not fair what's happened to us."

I decided to let them talk it out. I stood up. "I think I'll go get another dessert. I'll be right back."

As I was going through the line again, Wade came over. "Why are you sitting with them?"

"Because they're my friends."

"People are going to talk if you start associating with people like that."

"Look around you. How many of these people do we actually know? Would it kill us to talk to some of them once in a while?"

"If you hang out with losers, then you're a loser. It's as simple as that."

"I used to think that, but, you know what? It's not true."

Wade went back to the table with our friends. I figured they were probably talking about me, but I didn't care.

As I waited in line, I looked over at Emma Jean and Toby as they talked. Occasionally Toby would grab a paper napkin and blow his nose. *He's crying*, I thought. Normally I'm not in favor of guys crying, but I decided that maybe it was okay, especially if he's getting his feelings out in the open.

I got three extra desserts and went over to where Toby and Emma Jean were sitting.

"Anyone want an extra dessert?" I asked.

Toby sniffled. "I do."

"Here you go."

Toby enjoyed it so much that he ate Emma Jean's, too.

"Toby, do you ever wish you were involved in sports?" I asked.

"I'm not very good at sports."

"There are other things you can do."

"Like what?"

"Getting the uniforms ready for games. And being responsible for water. You'd be surprised how much water the team goes through during a game. The coaches are way too busy to worry about that. What would you think about giving us a hand? You get great seats for every game and you're part of the team."

Toby's eyes got big. "Are you serious?"

"Sure. Just before the rally starts today, come on by and I'll introduce you to the coaches, the trainer, and the students like you who help out."

Toby smiled. "Cool."

"You might also look at the school's sports Web page. That way you'll get to see the people you'll be meeting today."

Toby nodded and left.

"Emma Jean, can we talk about Saturday night?"

"What about it?"

I cleared my throat. "This is kind of embarrassing, but, do you remember me kissing you?"

"Yes."

"What do you think about that now?"

"The same thing I thought then. That you were only doing it because all the other girls had left. I just hoped you'd talk to me today, but I really didn't think you would." She paused. "I know how boys are."

I was surprised. "You do?"

"Yes. This happened one other time when I went to a party. And he never talked to me after that either."

"So, why do you go to parties?"

She shrugged her shoulders. "It's better than staying home and doing nothing."

"Well, I'm a little worried because—"

Before I could get it out, Madison came over to our table with a tray of food and sat down.

"Is it okay if I sit here?" she asked.

"Yeah, sure," I said.

Madison started eating. "Sorry to interrupt. Just go on."

I began to blush.

"Do you want me to go?" Madison asked.

"No, you're fine."

"We were talking about making out," Emma Jean said.

"What about it?"

I knew my face was getting red. "I met Emma Jean Saturday night at a party. After a while everyone left and we were sitting together on the couch watching a video of the game."

"Sounds fun."

"I kissed her a few times."

"I didn't know you guys were friends."

"We weren't."

"Oh." Madison paused. "So why were you making out with her?"

I wiped my forehead. "It was late, and I couldn't think of anything else to do."

Madison shot a disapproving glance at me.

"Nothing happened. She fell asleep, and after a while, I did too. It was really late. It was a mistake," I said. "Emma Jean, I didn't really care about you then."

Emma Jean had her gaze fastened on her empty dessert plate. "If you don't like me, why are you talking to me today?"

"Because you deserve better treatment than you got from me. I need to apologize for the way I treated you. What I did was wrong."

"If you know it was wrong today, why didn't you know it Saturday night?" Madison asked.

"Well, for one thing, I'd been drinking."

"That's not much of an excuse," Madison said.

"You're right. And . . ."

"What?" Madison asked.

"Well, the truth is, I've been thinking about what you said," I said to Madison.

"Me? What did I say?"

"Last Monday before the game when you interviewed me, you told me we're here on the earth to serve others. I've never had anyone say that to me."

"I find it hard to believe that my saying that to you could have had that much of an effect in your life."

"We've talked a lot."

"When?"

"Oh, sorry, you're right, just last Monday and today," I said.

Melissa came over to our table. "Cameron, I want to show you the cake we got for my uncle."

"I want to see it, too!" Madison said.

In the kitchen Melissa proudly showed off the cake. It was a beautiful sheet cake, decorated with musical notes and candy instruments.

"Who made this?" I asked.

"My mom got this lady at the bakery downtown to make it. She used the money we collected in class. My uncle is going to be so surprised! This was really a great idea."

I spent the rest of the day reading in the library about athletes who had made a difference by supporting a cause that benefitted people they cared about.

During the rally, as I introduced each member of the team, I made it a point to say something good about every one of them, not only their accomplishments on the field but some of the other ways they excelled in their lives.

Then it was time to introduce Jorge Gonzales.

"This is Jorge Gonzales," I said. "He transferred from another school, but he's been a vital part of our team. On the last play of the game, I had a choice. I could throw it to him because he was open and he never misses a pass thrown his way, or I could try to run it. I chose to run it, but if I had to do it all over again, I'd pass to Jorge because I know he'd catch it and run in for the touchdown. Let's hear it for Jorge Gonzales!"

I slapped Jorge on the shoulder as he came and stood next to me. "If anybody here has any relatives who work for a university, we need to make sure Jorge gets a football scholarship because he's an amazing player."

After the cheerleaders did their thing, I returned to the mic.

"One more thing before I turn it over to the coach. The band director, Mr. Walters, is retiring due to health reasons. In fact, this is his last day. Mr. Walters, could you come up here for a minute?"

Mr. Walters, totally surprised, walked sheepishly to the mic. I grabbed his hand, shook it, but then didn't let go. "Mr. Walters, on behalf of all the students who have been here during the time you've worked here, I'd like to thank you for brightening our days and making it fun to go to football and basketball games. We've prepared a little tribute to you."

The band played "Hail to the Chief". At the same time, two students rolled the cake out on a cart.

Representing the pep band, Madison gave a short talk about what a great experience it was to be led by Mr. Walters.

Another student came to the mic. "Mr. Walters, I couldn't help but notice you were conducting today without your baton. Did you lose it?"

"I did. I couldn't find it anywhere."

"Well, that's because we stole it! We were going to get it gold-plated, but actually that would have cost too much and we'd have never got it done in time, so instead we sprayed it with some gold spray paint." With a flourish, she pulled it from behind the podium. "So, here it is, Mr. Walters! You get the Gold Baton Award from the band!"

Everyone cheered. While the band played another song, Mr. Walters beamed with happiness, despite the tears streaming down his face.

Half an hour later the rally was over. Students poured out the doors and headed home.

Madison approached me. She seemed embarrassed.

We made eye contact. *She is so beautiful,* I thought. "Can I help you?" I asked.

"You're not at all the way I thought you'd be," she said.

I smiled. "I'm not at all the way I thought I'd be, either. And you know what? I owe it all to you."

"We only talked this morning."

"That's right. We've only had this Monday together. Even so, I've come to admire you a great deal."

She seemed uncomfortable at me saying that.

"Sorry," I added. "You probably don't know where that came from."

"No, I don't."

"Emma Jean has said a lot of good things about you."

"I see. Well, I'd better go."

"I'll see you tomorrow. I'll make it an even better day than today. You'll see. It's been a good day, but I'm pretty sure I can it make it even better. I want you to be proud of me."

"Why?"

"Because I respect you."

She seemed uncomfortable. "You don't even know me."

"I know you more than you could ever imagine."

"I really need to go," she said.

"I'll see you tomorrow."

As she left, I noticed one of the custodians coming in to clean up. "Need any help?" I asked.

"No thanks."

"This has been a great day," I said. "Do you mind if I just stay here for a few minutes?"

"No, not at all."

I sat down on one of the empty chairs. *What a change*, I thought. *At the beginning of this Monday, I was ready to do myself in and now I'm looking forward to the next Monday. I can do it better next time.*

A short time later, I headed for the door to leave the school. A second later, I returned involuntarily through the same door into the school.

Andy was there just like always. "Good luck tomorrow night, Cameron!" he called out.

I stopped in my tracks and turned to face him. "What'd you say?"

"Good luck tomorrow night in the game."

"What game?"

Andy laughed. "Yeah, right."

I studied the poster on the bulletin board. It read, "Go Eagles! Bring home the state trophy!"

"What day of the week is it?" I asked.

"It's Thursday."

"Thursday? Are you serious? Do you know what this means?"

"What?"

I began laughing. "It means I haven't yet made the mistakes I've already made!"

I ran down the hall with a huge smile on my face.

CHAPTER FIVE

In this version of Thursday I skipped all my classes so I could read about internet scams, but I did go to my eleven o'clock with Mrs. Arnold.

After class, I went up to her at her desk. "Mrs. Arnold?"

"Yes?"

"Don't send any more money. The whole thing is a scam."

She looked at me with a look of confusion in her eyes. "What are you talking about?"

"I know about the man in Nigeria who emailed you about the money. I know you've sent some money already and that today you're supposed to send thousands of dollars so he can wire the money to your account. Don't, okay? It's a scam. I looked it up online and printed this out for you. Please read it. They just want your money."

"What makes you think you know anything about my life?"

"I can't tell you how, but whatever you do, don't send the money. If you do, then by Monday, you'll be very depressed at having lost your life's savings."

"Please go, Cameron. I'm through talking with you. And in the future please stay out of my personal life."

"I can't do that. You have to go with me to the office so you can call the Better Business Bureau. I've got their number. Just call them, please."

She hesitated. "I guess that couldn't hurt anything."

She made the call and talked to them. I stood next to her while she explained what was happening to her.

By the time she hung up, she was crying.

I waited with her while she phoned her bank and froze her assets so that nobody could transfer any money out of her account.

Even so, I still worried that the next time I transitioned back in time, everything she'd done would be lost.

I caught up with Emma Jean and Toby in the cafeteria at the table where they usually ate.

I sat down with my tray of food. "How's it going?"

Emma Jean noticed my friends staring at me. "Are you lost?" she asked.

"Sometimes I get tired sitting with the same people all the time. And besides, you're a very pretty girl."

"No, I'm not."

"Well, I think you are. Look, if we win the game tomorrow night, then you might find out about a party Saturday night at Alexis' house. I know this sounds weird, but don't go."

"Why not?"

"Because sometimes a guy, especially after he's had a few beers, doesn't show respect for a girl he meets at a party. Look, if you want, maybe you, me, Toby, and Madison can have our own party at my place. My folks will be there. What do you think about that?"

"You have so many friends. I can't believe you'd want to spend time with us."

"Well, I just don't want you to get hurt, that's all."

"Okay."

"I'll call you Saturday about the party at my place. Okay?"

"I guess so."

"Toby, can I talk to you?" I asked.

"I guess."

"Coach Grogan asked me to talk with you. He really needs your help."

"I'm not very good at sports."

"It's okay. Come with me. You can leave your tray there and finish eating after we get back."

I took him to the equipment room. "Every time we have a game, when I go to suit up, everything I need is in my locker, and it's all clean. Without that, there would be no game. Who do you think takes care of all this? The coach?"

"I don't know."

"Well, the coach doesn't have time to do that. Instead, he has some student assistants who take care of the equipment."

We stopped in front of a large washer and dryer. "I don't know how many times they have to wash in one week. But I know none of the players ever has to worry about it. That's where you come in."

"Me?"

"Yeah, the coach wants you to work with him to do the behind-the-scenes work that keeps the football and the basketball programs going. Would you be willing to help us out?"

"I wouldn't know what to do."

"Mr. Collins, the assistant coach, and the other student assistants can teach you everything." I paused. "We need you, Toby."

For the first time, I saw a glimmer of life in his face as he said, "I guess I could do that."

"Of course you can. You'll be great!"

We were opening cupboards to see where everything was when a student assistant came in. "What are you guys doing?"

"Oh, you're just in time. Toby here is going to be helping you out from now on. Could you tell him how to do everything while I go talk to the coach?"

The coach's office door was closed.

I knocked.

"I'm busy!" the coach yelled.

I tried the door and walked in.

"Didn't I say I was busy?" he barked at me.

"You always say you're busy. I just recruited a student to help in the equipment room next season."

"Is that the job of a quarterback? No, it is not! I handpick all the assistants."

"Great. Could you please come out and handpick this kid? His name is Toby."

"Cameron, I swear, you're more trouble than you're worth."

"Toby's dad ditched his family so he's having kind of a hard time. I thought working with you, because you're such a great coach, might help him get through a rough patch."

He swore. "What am I? A social worker?"

"C'mon, Coach, it won't kill you to pay some attention to one kid, will it?"

"Since when did you get interested in someone besides yourself?"

"Since today. Let's go meet him. Show some of that southern

hospitality we've all come to appreciate in you."

He made a fist. "I'll southern hospitality you all the way down the hall if you don't get out of my office," the coach warned.

"Just meet the kid, Coach. That's all I'm asking. He's in the equipment room."

The coach threw down the report he was reading, stood up, and walked with me to the equipment room. "I liked it better when you were egotistical and selfish," he growled.

"What boy wouldn't love to hear one word of encouragement from a coach? And the good thing is it will only take a few minutes and yet it would mean so much to Toby. He doesn't have a dad in his life right now."

The coach looked at his watch. "Two minutes! That's all he gets."

"Oh, one more thing," I said.

"What?"

"I told him it was your idea to have him work for us."

The coach began pulling things out of his pocket and slapping them down in my hand. "Here's my car keys and my wallet. What else do you want? The nerve of you to come waltzing in, giving me orders, committing me to things I don't want to do. I'll be the happiest man in the world when you graduate."

I laughed. "I'll miss you, too, Coach."

We walked into the equipment room as one of the student assistants was explaining to Toby how to do laundry.

"I could do that!" Toby said with excitement in his voice.

"Toby, we're so glad you're going to help us out back here!" the coach said in the hearty, positive manner he usually reserved for parent groups. He shook Toby's hand. "Great to have you with us!

We'll talk later, but I just wanted to thank you. I'm sure you'll get things in great shape." Then he turned and walked back to his office.

"The kid shakes hands like a limp washrag," the coach complained privately to me as we walked back to his office.

"I'm sure you'll help him with that."

We paused at the door of the coach's office. "Anything else I can do for you?" the coach asked.

"Just one more thing. At practice today we need to work on some more pass plays involving Gonzales. The guy's amazing! He can catch anything. The key to us winning state is to work Gonzales into the game plan."

"Oh is that right? Since when do you come up with the game plan? We don't have time to work up new plays. I don't want to confuse the team."

"Okay, look, one pass play, that's all I'm asking. Gonzales will go long down the left side. I'll dodge the rush to buy some time and then I'll toss it as far as I can. I know him. He'll chase it down. Trust me."

The coach scowled. "I'm not promising anything, but maybe I'll consider it. You know what? Maybe someday I'll actually admit you played for us."

"Yeah, you will, Coach. I guarantee it."

The coach suppressed a grin and waved me off. "Yeah, yeah, see you at practice."

Half an hour later I spotted Madison in the hall. "Madison, I read what you wrote in the paper after our interview on Monday. You did a good job. But I need to fill you in on some preliminary information so you'll be able to write the story next Monday. It will only take a few minutes. How about in the library again?"

She shot me a distrustful glance but went with me anyway.

In the library, she took out a notebook and a pen. "What do you need to tell me?"

"I've noticed you lately. You go about your life quietly, doing what you can to help people." I struggled for what to say. "I've never respected a girl before, but I respect you. I find myself wanting to learn from you. I've learned so much already."

"You know what? There's something very weird going on. Excuse me." She stood up to leave.

"One more thing. I know this sounds crazy, but there's a small chance I might be falling for you."

She panicked. "I really need to go." She got up and walked out of the library.

I caught up with her. "That was way over the top, wasn't it? I'll do better next time."

"There won't be a next time."

I smiled. "That's where you're wrong. There's always a next time. Except you won't remember it. Excuse me. I have to start Thursday over again. I'll do better next time. For one thing I won't tell you I'm falling for you."

I excused myself, hurried to the outside door, and a short time later was forced back into the school to start another Thursday.

I ran past Andy who yelled something at me.

I found Madison standing outside my locker.

"Can we do a follow-up interview now?" she asked. "I know you'll be busy later on. Especially with the victory rally this afternoon." She pulled out her notebook. "This is a big day for you, isn't it?"

"No, no, that's what you say on Monday."

"This is Monday."

"No, it isn't. This is Thursday."

"Did you get hit during the game?"

"The game? The game hasn't been played."

"Yes it has. You made the winning touchdown."

"No, that's totally wrong! I passed to Gonzales. He made the touchdown."

She pulled a copy of the local newspaper out of her backpack. "That's not what it says here."

"That can't be! There must be some mistake."

"For you personally, what was it like to win the state football title?"

"Is it really Monday?"

"It is."

"That means I didn't pass to Gonzales on the last play."

"No, you ran the ball in for a touchdown."

"That means that today Mrs. Arnold will realize she's lost her life's savings on a scam. I was so close to helping her keep her money."

She stopped writing. "Actually, I don't think I'll put any of this in the paper."

"I can explain everything."

"Okay."

"For a while I kept repeating Monday over and over again, and then suddenly I was back to Thursday. And that was great. I was so happy."

"Why?"

"Think about what it would be like to go back in time and fix all your mistakes. Not to do the things you feel guilty about. Aren't there a few things you wish you'd never done?"

She paused. "Yes, I do have regrets. Things I wish I'd never done."

"I guess most people do, right?"

"I don't know about most people. I only know about myself."

"What if I tell you that I want to learn more about what you believe?"

"Why?"

"Just curious, I guess."

"You're serious?"

"Yeah, I am."

"I guess I could arrange that. I'd have to make a few phone calls is all. How would at my house after school work for you?"

"That might be a problem," I said. "See, the thing is, I'm finding it difficult to leave school."

"Do you or do you not want to learn about what I believe?"

"I do."

"Then I'll meet you at your locker after the pep rally."

I sighed. "I guess."

That afternoon I did the pep rally the same way as the last time, except I spent more time praising my team members by name.

After the rally I posed for pictures with Mr. Walters and the band and then I went to my locker, where Madison was waiting for me.

She started toward the outside door.

I froze in place.

She stopped and looked back at me. "You coming?"

I caught up with her as we walked to the exit. I stopped in front of the first of the two doors leading to the parking lot. "Wait a second. Hold my hand Madison."

She shook her head. "I don't know you well enough for that."

"Let me tell you what's going to happen. At first there will be a light and then a big wind that will make it impossible for me to reach the outer door. And then I'll be blown back into the school and back to Monday."

She looked at me skeptically. "Yeah, right."

I took a deep breath, grabbed her hand anyway, and together we pushed through both sets of doors.

And suddenly we were both outside the school.

CHAPTER SIX

Nothing had happened, and now Madison and I were both outside the school, with me still holding her hand.

She scowled at me and pulled her hand away. "What's going on? I told you I didn't want to hold hands with you."

Totally overcome emotionally, I sat down on the steps. "I didn't think this would ever happen."

"What? That some girl wouldn't want to hold your hand?"

"No, that I'd ever get out of the school. I've tried so many times, but each time a big wind blew me back in the school, and it would always be Monday morning."

"What are you talking about?"

I looked up at her. There was no way I could ever explain this in such a way that she'd believe me. "Nothing. It was just a metaphor."

She nodded. "I like metaphors."

"I could've guessed that. Now that I'm out, I'm not sure what to do."

"We're going to my house so people from my church can teach you. I've set it all up."

"I'm sorry. I've had such a long day. I think I'd better just go home."

"No problem. Maybe some other time, okay?" She paused. "So I guess I'll see you around."

"Yeah, I guess." I stood up. "Can I give you a ride home?"

"See that house on the hill? That's where I live. I usually walk home, but thanks for the offer."

"Okay, then. I guess I'll go home. It's been a long time since I've seen my mom and dad. Oh, thanks for all your help. You've been a big help to me all through this."

"Through all what?"

"Today."

"What did I do?"

I sighed. "More than you'll ever know."

She shrugged. "Okay, if you say so."

"Please let me give you a ride home."

"Okay, if you insist."

As we pulled out of the parking lot onto the street, she turned to me and asked, "Why does a football hero want to give someone like me a ride home?"

"I've been thinking that it might be good if I were more like you. You're friends with everyone. I'm not like that, but now I'm beginning to think that maybe I should be. Why do you care about people so much?"

She paused as if she were trying to decide what to say. Finally, she said softly, "I believe that because God loves us, we should love others."

That freaked me out. I pulled into her driveway. "Okay, well, maybe I'll see you tomorrow."

"Maybe so."

As I drove home, at first I thought about telling my mom everything that had happened to me that day, but by the time I walked through the door, I'd changed my mind. Knowing my mom, she'd have me examined for a brain tumor. So I decided not to tell her.

When I'd been stuck at school, I pictured that if I were ever able to return home, I'd give my mom a big hug and tell her how much I love and appreciate her. But now that I was free to come and go, I'd lost that feeling. Also, any insight I'd gained while repeating the same day over and over seemed to be slipping away.

"Hi, Mom," I said, grabbing an apple and heading for my room.

"How was your day?" she asked.

I suppressed a smile. "Long. Very long."

I was halfway to my room when I retraced my steps to add, "Oh, USC is considering me. The coach is going to call me tonight."

"USC? That's your first choice, isn't it?"

"Yeah, I guess so," I said weakly.

"You don't sound very happy about it."

"I'm just tired, that's all. Like I said, it's been a long day."

In my room I watched local news coverage of the game that our neighbors had recorded Friday night. The sports guy showed me holding the trophy high in the air and giving a victory shout.

That's what I want out of life, I thought. *To be the best and to have the best. The best cars, the best apartments, and the best women. That's what life is all about.*

As I thought about what I was going to say when the USC coach called, I thought about suggesting he take a look at Jorge Gonzales, too. At first it seemed like the right thing to do, but then I began wondering how that would go over with the coach. If I were to do that, the coach might just tell me to forget the whole thing, and I really wanted to play for USC. So I decided not to say anything about Gonzales.

At seven o'clock the coach from USC did call. After a brief conversation about us winning the state football title, he said, "We'd like to fly you out in a few weeks for an on-campus visit. I can have my secretary make all the arrangements."

"That sounds great. I look forward to meeting you," I said.

When I got off the phone, instead of being happy, I felt disappointed in me.

But only momentarily. *I'm not responsible for Gonzales,* I thought. *I'm not responsible for anyone. Just me.*

I was exhausted after my long day and fell asleep a little after eight-thirty.

But I woke up a little before ten o'clock.

I got out of bed and went to my window. *What's wrong with me?* I thought. *Did I learn nothing from what I've been through? Am I going to go through the rest of my life being a self-centered jerk? I couldn't say one decent word to USC about Gonzales? Will I go to school tomorrow and completely ignore Madison and Emma Jean and Toby?"*

And then it got worse. I went back in my mind to all the times I'd used or ignored or mocked people. It seemed to me I'd gone through my life with no thought about anyone else except myself.

I put my shoes on, grabbed my keys, and headed for the garage. My mom and dad were still up.

"Where are you going?" my mom asked.

"Back to school. I left something in my locker. I need to get it."

"The school will be closed by now."

"If it is, I'll come back."

The school was still open because of a student play that night.

I went inside through the same door I always used. And then I turned and faced the door.

Maybe it will work this time. Maybe when I try to go outside, I'll be pushed back inside and it will be a Monday from last month or a year ago and I'll be able to erase the mistakes I made that day. And maybe if I do it enough times, I'll quit being such a jerk all the time.

I walked outside and stopped. Nothing had happened. *It didn't work,* I thought.

I went back inside and then came out again.

It still didn't work. Maybe next time.

I did this over and over again, and each time nothing happened.

I went in. I went out. I went in. I went out.

And each time I became more desperate. And the burden of all the cruel, unkind, selfish, and stupid things I'd done to others kept running through my mind.

What is going on? Why is this happening to me?

After about ten minutes, though, as I was coming out of the school for about the hundredth time, Madison was standing there, watching me.

"Cameron? You okay?" she asked.

"Yeah, sure. I forgot something in my locker, and I went to go get it."

"I was in our kitchen getting a drink of water, and I looked out the window and saw you going in and out of the school over and over again."

I knew my face was turning red.

"You want to talk?" she asked.

"Yeah, I guess."

"My dad brought me here. He's in our car. Would you like to meet him?"

"Sure."

She led me to where their car was parked. Her dad got out of the car.

"Dad, this is Cameron."

We shook hands. "Good to meet you," I said.

"Dad, Cameron and I need to talk for a few minutes. Is it okay if I have him bring me home?"

"Yes, as long as you're not too late. You have school in the morning."

"I know."

"I'll have her home in thirty minutes," I promised.

"Okay." He turned to her. "I'll wait up for you."

We watched her dad drive away.

"In ninth grade," I began, "I accused a guy in school of doing something I knew he hadn't done, just so I'd have an excuse to fight him."

"Why did you do that?"

"Because I liked to beat people up."

"Oh."

I sighed. "You know what? I'm not proud of doing that. If I could go back in time to that very day, I'd leave him alone."

"Well, that's good, you know, that you've matured."

"It was not, like, gradual. This all happened Monday."

"Well, at least it happened, right?"

"Yeah, I guess. But here's the thing. I've been selfish and conceited and arrogant my whole life. So what's going to keep me from reverting back to that again?"

"You need something I've had all my life."

"What is it?"

"My faith in Jesus Christ."

'I'm not into religion. I'm more practical."

"This is practical. It's just something you work on every day. Even though we've all made mistakes, we can start over and try to do better next time. Once you make changes in your life, the regret and the guilt goes away. Jesus makes that possible."

I laughed. "That sounds too easy."

"Well, it's not that easy because sometimes you have to go back to people you've hurt and apologize and ask for their forgiveness. That's hard to do."

I nodded. "I think I could do that."

"I believe you could."

"What else do you have to do?" I asked.

"Work on becoming the kind of person who would never do what you have done."

"That's the hard part, right?"

"Yeah, it is. It takes effort every day. But it's worth it."

"I think I want that in my life."

"Good. Let me set it up again."

"Okay, if you'll be there with me."

"I will. I promise."

"When can we do this?" I asked.

"Let me see if I can set up a time after school tomorrow. Maybe at my house. How would that be for you?"

"That should be good."

"Okay then. Why don't you take me home?"

At her door, I thought about giving her a hug, but I didn't because she would think we'd only known each other one day. But I'd actually known her much longer than that. Long enough to have gained respect and admiration for her.

CHAPTER SEVEN

When I entered the school Tuesday morning, I was actually relieved it wasn't Monday again and that Andy wasn't there to tell me I'd played a good game. He wasn't anywhere to be seen.

Not only that, but as I walked down the hall to my locker, not only did nobody tell me what a great game I'd had, but also I didn't actually recognize anyone either.

I had trouble getting my locker open. The combination didn't seem to work even though I tried it five or six times.

A guy came up and stood next to me as he watched me try the combination again. "What are you doing?" he asked.

"Trying to get my locker opened."

"That's actually my locker."

I checked the locker number again. "No it isn't."

"It is. Here, I'll prove it to you." He stepped up to the locker, did the combination, and opened the door.

None of my things were in the locker.

"Something's wrong," I said.

The guy shrugged. "I wouldn't know about that, but I do know this is my locker."

"I need to find Madison. She'll help me. She always helps me."

"You're not a student here."

"What are you talking about? Of course I am. I'm the quarterback of the football team. We just won the state championship."

He laughed. "Yeah, right. This year we didn't even make it to the playoffs. Look, I hate to burst your bubble, but you're way too old to be in high school."

I backed away from him. "You know what? I need to go out the door and come back in again."

As I started toward the outside door, two men in suits saw me and hurried toward me. "We're so sorry! We thought you'd come in the main entrance so we were waiting there."

One of them shook my hand. "I'm Douglas Baxter, the principal. I talked to you on the phone. And this is my assistant, Roger Atkinson. Let's go to my office and talk. We're so happy you agreed to come here and talk to our students. It's not often we get such a distinguished graduate to come back. The students are excited that you'll be here today. All the boys in school know who you are and many of the girls do also."

He stopped just outside his office. "Just one thing. We're hoping you can somehow avoid talking about your pending divorce. I'm sure you regret, as we do, that your wife has been doing the talk-show route, telling what we hope are lies about what she calls your outrageous behavior on road trips."

"I'm married?"

"Well, as you know, it's still tied up in the courts. According to CNN, nothing happened overnight so my guess is you're still married."

I wiped my sweating forehead. "There's a student here I need to talk to. Her name is Madison."

"Why do you need to talk to her?"

"She always knows what to say to make me feel better."

The two men looked at each other strangely, no doubt wondering why a married man would want to go to a high-school girl for advice.

"Actually, she's my . . . uh . . . er, cousin . . . niece," I added.

I happened to look at the calendar. It was ten years ahead of time. I panicked. "Excuse me. I need to use the restroom," I stammered.

"Just through that door."

I stumbled into the faculty bathroom, turned on the light, and looked at myself in the mirror. Except it wasn't me. It was someone older and much bulkier than me. "No, this isn't happening! This can't be happening."

I doused my face with water, dried off, and came out of the office again. "Look, I left something in my car that I need to get. Can you excuse me for a second?"

I didn't even wait for their answer. I knew I had to first see if I could get out or if I'd be trapped in the future for days at a time.

As I staggered to the door, I saw the lights again and heard the wind. After I'd made it through the first door I pushed with all my might and somehow made it through the second set of doors. As I staggered forward, I fell onto the ground and must have passed out for a moment.

When I awoke, I found myself lying face up on the ground. It was night-time, and the witch from my dreams with the silver magic wand in her hand was staring down at me.

The trainer for the team knelt beside me. "Cameron, how are you doing?"

I panicked. "Why is there a witch here?"

The trainer called out. "We need to get him to the ER!"

I don't remember anything that happened after that.

I woke up in a bed, but not my bed, and Madison was sitting in a chair near the foot of the bed reading something.

I didn't want her to know I was awake until I figured out what was going on. Without moving my head, I glanced at my surroundings. *I must be in the hospital. But why?*

And then I remembered the last play of the game, when I got tackled. But just being tackled shouldn't have put me in the hospital. So what had happened?

Madison closed her book, closed her eyes, and began reciting something: "And now, after the many testimonies that have been given of him, this is the testimony, last of all, which we give of him: That he lives! For we saw him, even on the right hand of God; and we heard the voice bearing record that he is the only begotten of the Father—that by him, and through him, and of him, the worlds are and were created, and the inhabitants thereof are begotten sons and daughters unto God."

She went back to her book to make sure she'd said it correctly, then made a check on a piece of paper and continued reading.

I studied her face.

There is something about her. It isn't that she is drop-dead gorgeous. If I came up with a list of the fifty hottest girls in school, she wouldn't even make the cut. The clothes she wears aren't at all sexy. She doesn't seem desperate to get a guy to notice her. She's never been to any of the parties I've gone to. I wonder what she actually does on the weekends.

I continued to look at her. *She's not a girl I'd pick to show her off to my friends because they'd think she's hot. And yet there's something about her that draws me to her. I wonder what it is? It has nothing to do with things like makeup or jewelry or the way she does her hair. And yet, it makes me feel better just seeing her sitting there. To me it shows that she cares about what happened to me.*

So what possible use could she ever be to me, and why am I watching her every move and listening to her try to memorize something from the Bible?

She has nothing that I look for in a girl. I like girls who think that being with me will impress their friends. But she's clearly not that stupid.

Instead of thinking of some way to impress her, I . . . I feel . . . inferior to her. That's it. She's too good for me. I'm too shallow, too conceited, too egotistical for someone like her.

Why should I waste my time with a girl I respect? If I did, before long she'd be calling all the shots, and that's just not right. I always have to be the one in charge. I'm a star quarterback for the number one high school football team in the state. I'm not going to have some girl telling me what to do.

She closed her book, keeping one finger on a page so she could go back to it again, and began reciting what she'd memorized.

What is going on here? There is no reason I should have anything more to do with this girl. She would never get drunk with me. She wouldn't put out for me. I can't show her off to my friends. So what other reason is there to be with a girl?

And then it came to me. *We could be friends.*

A girl who is also a friend? That was a novel thought for me. *Maybe she could help me be a better person. She could show me how to be friends with people like Emma Jean or Toby or the band geeks.*

One thing I know for sure about Madison: My mom would love her.
That would be a first for me.

She's beautiful, though, just not in a way I've ever considered. The
goodness that's in her is what makes her beautiful. She's virtuous, lovely,
and of good report. I paused. *Whatever that means.*

She glanced up from her book and saw that I was staring at her.

She stood up and came over to me. She was smiling. "You're
awake?"

"I hope so."

"You know what? I'll go get a nurse."

"No. Wait a minute." I needed to know if I had only been
dreaming. "Why were you on the football field standing over me?"
I asked.

"I wasn't on the football field. When you got tackled you were
near the sidelines. You got up, stumbled, and ran into one of the
light poles. You landed face up on the running track. The pep band
was on the track, on our way back to the bus when it happened, so
you landed right next to me. You looked at my flute and got this
scared look on your face. And then the trainers and the doctors
came and told me to get out of the way. So I left."

"So you're the witch with the magic wand, right?"

She faked it. "Yeah, right. You know what? I should go get a
nurse."

I desperately tried to make sense of what she was saying.

"Wait. Tell me something. What day is it?" I asked.

"It's Monday. You've been in a coma since you got hurt Friday
night."

I got a big grin on my face. "I should have known. It's always
Monday."

She reached into her backpack and pulled out her cell phone. "Let me call your mom and dad. I came between classes to see what I could find out about your condition so I could write about it for the school paper. Your mom and dad had been here the whole time, and they looked so tired, I offered to watch you so they could go home and get some sleep. They've been gone about two hours."

She made the call. "Hello, guess what? Good news! Cameron's awake! Yes, I'll tell him you're on your way."

She ended the call. "They'll be right over."

"So, I didn't make a touchdown on the last play?"

"No. You threw a pass just before you got tackled."

"Who to?"

"I think his last name is Gonzales."

"What'd he do with it?"

"After he caught it, he made a touchdown."

"So we won?"

"Yes. You guys are the state football champions."

I couldn't help grinning. "That's great! Jorge will be able to get a football scholarship then. I'm glad for him."

I reached for her hand, but she pulled away just a little. "Please. I'm so sick," I begged.

She nodded and relaxed and let me hold her hand.

Suddenly I realized that the only time we'd actually talked was when she interviewed me the Monday before the game. Everything else was the product of a frenzied mind as I lay unconscious in the hospital.

"I dreamt about you while I was out."

"You did? What did you dream?"

"A lot of things. All good. About how you go out of your way to be friends with everyone in school. Also that you're virtuous, lovely, and a good reporter."

I was freaking her out. She pulled her hand away, went to the window, and looked out for my folks while I tried to put things together. "Your mom and dad just pulled in. They'll be here in a minute. They're going to be so happy to see you awake."

"Before they get here, I need to ask you a question," I said.

"Okay."

I didn't know what to say. *Can I be your friend? No, that will freak her out.*

Can you show me how to become a better person? She'd never believe that coming from me. She must have heard all the bad-boy stories that have circulated around school about me. She'd immediately be suspicious of my motives if I said that.

You're the kind of girl my mom hopes will some day be the mother of my children? Even though it was true, saying it would be such a colossal mistake. She'd go running and screaming out of the room if I say that.

"You're going to ask me a question, right?" she asked.

"Yes."

"What is your question?"

I sighed. Once again it was fourth down with only a few seconds on the clock. It was up to me to put up or shut up.

Finally it came to me. "Do you think it's still possible to get that free Christmas DVD?"

I don't know why that made her so happy, but she gave me a huge smile and said, "I think I can arrange that."

That's all I needed. That's all any quarterback needs. Just an opening. Just a lane. Just a tiny fraction of time that can change things forever. Things like winning a high school football title. Or even, maybe, changing your life.

That's possibly what I'd accomplished with my question.

Time would tell.

The next day I was released from the hospital. I stayed home from school the rest of the week.

I went to church with Madison on Sunday. During Sunday school, the elders taught me the first discussion. One of them had played football in high school so we had something in common.

The next Monday I returned to school. Nothing much happened except that it rained all day. Most people went about their lives in the same way they always did, with very little change in themselves or their surroundings, having the same attitudes and making the same mistakes they'd made on previous days with nothing really changing.

But, in addition to the rain, Monday was different for me in one major way. Because of my growing understanding of what Jesus Christ has done for all of us, I felt like this could be the beginning of a new life for me. Hopefully with Madison always in my life, but if not, then with someone just like her.

So what I'm trying to say is that, for me at least, it was an awesome day.

ABOUT THE AUTHOR:

Jack Weyland is one of the best-known authors of young adult fiction for Latter-day Saint audiences, having written over twenty best selling novels. His first novel *Charly* was made into a movie in 2002. For further information, go to www.jackweyland.com.

ALSO AVAILABLE FROM JACK WEYLAND

The Samaritan Bueno

Dan and his two friends are asked to deliver a food box to a needy family. By mistake they deliver it to the wrong house and meet Maria, an undocumented mom and her two young kids. Over the next few weeks, Dan becomes drawn into Maria's life, his parents find themselves at a loss to deal with his uncharacteristic behavior.

In this thought-provoking, tender, and humorous novel, Jack Weyland tackles timely and difficult issues.